RAGTAG

RAGTAG

KARL WOLF-MORGENLÄNDER

CLARION BOOKS
Houghton Mifflin Harcourt
Boston ✦ New York
2009

Clarion Books
215 Park Avenue South, New York, New York 10003
Copyright © 2009 by Karl Wolf-Morgenländer
Illustrations copyright © 2009 by Tim Jessell

The illustrations were executed in digital oils using Corel Painter X.
The text was set in 11.5-point Figural Book.
Map by Kayley LeFaiver.

Clarion Books is an imprint of
Houghton Mifflin Harcourt Publishing Company.

www.clarionbooks.com

Printed in the United States of America

Library of Congress Cataloging-in-Publication Data

Wolf-Morgenländer, Karl.
Ragtag / Karl Wolf-Morgenländer.
p. cm.
Summary: A young swallow leads a band of birds against an empire of
raptors that has invaded Boston.
ISBN 978-0-547-07424-5
[1. Birds—Fiction. 2. Birds of prey—Fiction. 3. War—Fiction. 4. Boston
(Mass.)—Fiction.] I. Title.

PZ7.W81935Rag 2009
[Fic]—dc22

2008025319

MP 10 9 8 7 6 5 4 3 2 1

To my parents, for their unwavering support

CONTENTS

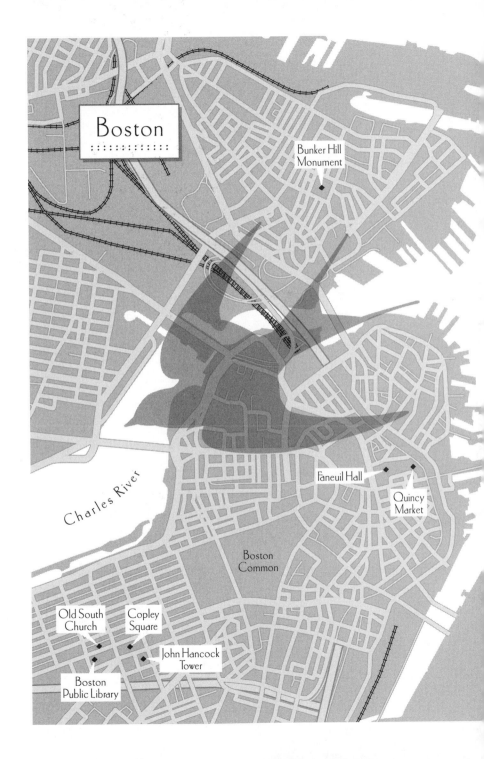

Boston
: : : : : : : : : : : : : :

Bunker Hill
Monument

Faneuil Hall

Quincy
Market

Charles River

Boston
Common

Old South
Church

Copley
Square

John Hancock
Tower

Boston
Public Library

RAGTAG

Where's Ragtag? Blue Feather wondered as she gazed from her perch high atop the belfry of the Old South Church. A brisk wind picked up, blowing through the narrow streets of Boston's Copley Square. The swallow shivered as the wind ruffled her feathers. She hopped from foot to foot, trying in vain to keep warm. She could sense that the wind was only the beginning. Behind the twinkling lights of the city lay a shadow darker than night. It was only a matter of time until the storm arrived.

Amid the dark clouds, birds of every shape and size were zeroing in on the church. Gulls, pigeons, finches, blue jays, and robins all landed on the narrow ledge around the belfry. Each one nodded to Blue Feather before quickly hopping inside.

A cardinal named Proud Beak fluttered down next to the swallow. He folded his crimson wings and took a few steps toward the interior before turning back. "Aren't you coming?"

Blue Feather shook her head. "I'm waiting for Ragtag."

"*Hmmph.* You'll be waiting all night," Proud Beak retorted. "That child of yours is always late. He only thinks of himself. And on tonight of all nights! It's a disgrace."

"He'll be here."

"A mother's optimism is never-ending. Where's Bobtail?"

"Looking for Ragtag."

"Typical. How he puts up with his younger brother, I'll never know."

A cold gust sprang up, ruffling both birds' feathers.

"The storm's close," Proud Beak said. "I'm going in, and you'd better, too. Hoogol will be arriving soon, and tonight we have much to discuss. The Talon Empire is advancing faster than we thought. The clans may not be able to hold the city. . . ."

Proud Beak's voice trailed off as he realized that Blue Feather's attention was elsewhere. He impatiently tapped a claw on the ledge. "Blue Feather, are you listening?"

"I hear you. Why don't you go on ahead?"

"You're the leader of the swallows! You should be inside with the others, not waiting out here for that irresponsible child of yours."

"I'll be in soon. I promise." Blue Feather tried her best to ignore the cardinal's look of disapproval as he turned to go inside. Proud Beak's position in the Feathered Alliance—the loose coalition of clans that governed the birds of Boston—was second only to Hoogol's. And Proud Beak made sure nobody ever forgot that.

The wind grew stronger, forcing Blue Feather to hop back. Her forked tail twitched nervously as she kept her eyes on the ragged clouds.

One by one, the leaders of the chickadees, the mourning doves, the starlings, the woodpeckers, and the blackbirds fluttered down to the ledge next to her and entered the belfry.

A brown-and-black-feathered sparrow named Tattler

suddenly zoomed out of the darkness, struggling against the wind as she landed next to Blue Feather. She was small and stocky, with a dark smudge on her breast band.

"Of all the nights for Hoogol to call a meeting," the sparrow muttered as she tried in vain to smooth her pearl-white tail feathers.

"Any sign of Ragtag?" Blue Feather asked.

"No luck so far," Tattler replied. "Bobtail and I have been searching for him for the last hour or so, but we split up to cover more ground."

Blue Feather looked out over the city. As her eyes fell on a ribbon of darkness that she knew was the Charles River, she thought about what Proud Beak had said.

"Is it true?" she asked. "About the birds of prey massing along the far side of the river?"

Tattler hesitated. "It's true. A few have made scouting raids into the city, but don't worry. Ragtag's heard the news. I'm sure he's smart enough to stay away from the river." She glanced into the belfry. A crowd of birds was huddled near the large bell, anxiously talking. "I'd better head in. Hoogol will be arriving soon, and he'll want my report."

Blue Feather continued to watch the sky over Boston as the sparrow hopped inside. She trembled at the thought of the Talon Empire—hundreds of birds of prey who were even now gathering in strength along the northern banks of the Charles. What would happen to the Feathered Alliance?

The swallow shivered as she was hit with a blast of wind

from the east, bringing with it the smell of rain. She could think of only one thing as a flash of lightning in the distance promised worse to come.

Where was Ragtag?

Ragtag

A Swallow Named Ragtag

Ragtag spread his wings to slow his descent as he glided toward the roof of the Boston Public Library. He fluttered to a landing, then quickly hopped onto a ledge overlooking Copley Square. The wind increased, almost knocking him over.

There's a storm coming, Ragtag thought as he peered at the Old South Church across the street. He couldn't see the belfry in the darkness, but he knew it was filled with birds. The swallow felt a momentary pang of regret. No doubt his mother was waiting for him. He could almost feel her eyes staring down at him.

He shuddered as he thought of the council meetings. As the son of a clan leader, he knew it was his duty to attend, yet he could never figure out why. Nobody ever bothered to listen to him. The last time Ragtag had gone to a council meeting, he'd fallen asleep and started to snore, much to Proud Beak's annoyance. He could still remember the verbal lashing the cardinal had given him.

"That's it, I'm not going," Ragtag muttered to himself as a flash of lightning lit the sky. For a second, he wavered. He knew the Feathered Alliance was in a panic over the approaching birds of prey. Perhaps it was a bit selfish of him not to attend. He shook himself, irritated at his own indecision. Whatever the clan leaders decided, they could decide without him. What good was worrying?

Having made up his mind, he was about to take flight when his older brother, Bobtail, suddenly fluttered down next to him.

"There you are!" Bobtail said. "I've been looking all over the city for you. Come on, we're late enough as it is."

"I'm not going," Ragtag replied.

"What? What do you mean?"

Ragtag shrugged his wings. "I mean I'm not coming. I've had it with council meetings. They're boring, just a bunch of stuffy old birds sitting around talking endlessly. I've got better things to do."

"Of all the nerve!" Bobtail sputtered, his tail twitching anxiously. "I've wasted the last hour searching for you, thinking you were lost or needed help, and all this time you've just been avoiding your responsibilities. You impudent, immature—"

"Who are you calling immature?"

"You! You only think of yourself. Sometimes I'm amazed that we're brothers."

"You're not the only one." Ragtag watched as his brother started preening. "Will you stop that? Your feathers are fine. You're always fussing over your appearance. I don't know why you even bother."

"There's nothing wrong with looking your best," Bobtail protested with a sniff, then cast a critical eye on his younger brother. "You should try it sometime. You look like last year's nest. It's embarrassing having you around."

"Well, I can solve that problem." Ragtag took flight and soared over to a chimney on the far side of the roof. He didn't bother to turn around to see if Bobtail had followed; he knew that if there was one thing Bobtail hated, it was to lose an argument. Even worse was to lose to his younger brother.

"You're a fool, Ragtag!" Bobtail said as he landed next to him. "Just for once, I wish you would stop thinking of yourself. Haven't you heard about the birds of prey? If we don't do anything—"

"What are we going to do?" Ragtag asked. "I'll tell you: nothing! If the Talon Empire wants to overrun the city, they'll overrun it. Who's going to stop them? Hoogol? He's too old. The council? All they do is sit around and talk."

"Proud Beak says—"

"Oh, not again!" Ragtag interrupted. "Proud Beak says this and Proud Beak says that! Yak yak yak!"

"You should listen to him," Bobtail retorted. "He cares about our future. The only thing you seem to care about is yourself."

"That's not true. I just don't waste time worrying about things I can't control. You should try it sometime. Life's too short."

"Hardly! One day I'll be the leader of the Feathered Alliance. Then it'll be *my* worrying that helps us."

Ragtag couldn't help snickering. "The leader of the Feathered Alliance? You? No swallow has ever been elected to lead the alliance!"

Bobtail puffed up his feathers. "Proud Beak says I have the makings of a true leader."

"Here we go again," Ragtag said. "Proud Beak says this and Proud Beak says that. It's pathetic how you always grovel around him. Everyone else thinks so, too. You should hear the clan leaders talk when you're not around."

This was too much for Bobtail. With a loud squawk, he plowed into his younger brother. The two swallows pecked angrily at each other as they rolled across the roof—a whirlwind of feathers, claws, and snapping beaks.

Ragtag finally managed to break free and fluttered his wings in his brother's face, forcing him to back off.

"Go on, get out of here!" Ragtag yelled. "Go to your stupid little meeting."

"Fine! Fly your own way, like you always do," Bobtail declared, and launched himself from the library's roof.

Ragtag watched him vanish toward the Old South Church; then he, too, took flight and headed north. He quickly gained altitude as the wind picked up. Let Bobtail go huddle with the clan leaders in that dusty old belfry, he thought. I'm going to play.

High above the streets, the swallow folded his wings and plunged toward the ground. The rooftops rushed at him. At the very last moment, he spread his wings and allowed an updraft to carry him back to the clouds.

Ragtag dipped and dove, catching insects as he played on the winds preceding the storm. Longfellow Bridge suddenly loomed in the darkness. He dropped like a rock, soared beneath it, then glided out the other side.

The clan leaders don't know what they're missing, Ragtag thought as he hit an updraft and gained altitude. Wild nights were grand. There was nothing more exhilarating than surfing the gales before a storm.

A light from below caught his eye, and he dropped lower out of curiosity. A half-dozen humans wearing orange jackets were searching the riverbank with lights. Ragtag landed atop a streetlamp and watched as they moved past, talking in their strange language.

Sheets of rain suddenly began to cascade from the clouds. The swallow quickly lost interest in the humans and looked around for shelter. The silhouette of an abandoned factory was visible in the darkness a short distance away. He made a beeline for a broken window on the top floor, but just as he reached it, he realized he was flying way too fast.

Ragtag desperately fluttered his wings in an attempt to land upright. His claws hit the floor, but the rest of him kept going, and he tumbled end over end until he finally slid to a stop against a wall. How embarrassing, he thought as he jumped to his feet and shook out his feathers. He could just imagine Bobtail's laughter.

Shadows crowded around him, and the sound of the rain echoed through the cavernous space. A flash of lightning lit up the vast chamber. Old machines covered in dust were strewn throughout the attic. It was a creepy place, but at least he was out of the weather.

Ragtag hopped over to the window and gazed down at

the riverbank. He could just make out the humans with their lights. He cocked his head to one side and watched as they slowly made their way toward the factory. What were humans doing outside on a night like this?

A howling wind blew rain through the shattered glass. Realizing he had no choice but to wait out the storm, the swallow looked around for a comfortable spot. Just as he had settled himself and his eyes were slipping closed, he heard an ominous rustle that made his blood run cold.

He wasn't alone.

Baldur

The Monster in the Attic

Ragtag whirled, wings poised, ready to take flight. "Hello?" he called, his voice quavering. He peered through the darkness, wondering if a cat could have somehow found its way into the attic. Lightning flashed, and thunder rumbled in the distance. The swallow waited with a pounding heart. Once again, he heard a strange rustling in the shadows.

He glanced at the broken windows, wondering if he should risk taking to the air. He knew it wasn't safe to venture out in a downpour. It was hard to see the city's skyscrapers through the rain, and it would only take one strong gust to blow him into a wall.

"Hello?" Ragtag said again. "Is anyone here?" He tried to make his voice confident and bold, but it emerged a bit shaky. He hopped forward cautiously. If there was one thing he couldn't stand, it was a mystery.

A voice suddenly rang out. "If you come any closer, I'll rip you to shreds."

Ragtag quickly fluttered back to the safety of the window. He peered down at the dark space behind the crates where the voice had come from, ready to fly at the first sign of an approaching predator. The lightning continued to flash while the thunder roared and the rain pounded with unrelenting intensity. No further sound emerged from the darkness.

Ragtag lowered his wings. Every instinct told him to take flight, but his curiosity held him in place. He wasn't about to fly for his life like a terrified pigeon just because of some voice in the shadows.

"Why are you hiding?" Ragtag yelled as he puffed up his feathers to make himself look bigger. "Show yourself!" There was no response. He jumped to the floor and hopped forward. "That is," he added, "unless you're afraid. . . ."

A shadow suddenly loomed out of the darkness at the same time that a bolt of lightning lit the attic. Ragtag screamed as a massive bald eagle rushed toward him with outstretched wings and an open beak! Just as it was about to reach him, the giant raptor jerked to a stop and fell flat. The swallow scrambled back and huddled in a corner, too terrified to fly away.

The eagle lay where it had fallen. After a few seconds, Ragtag was able to control himself long enough to look at it. There was a strange object wrapped around one of the eagle's legs. It looked metallic and had a flashing red light. A small cord attached to it was wedged between a crack in the floorboards. The giant bird was trapped.

Wearily the eagle lifted its head and stared at Ragtag. A look of relief appeared on its face.

"Thank goodness," the eagle said, his voice full of exhaustion. "It's only a little sparrow."

"I'm a swallow!" Ragtag corrected him indignantly.

"Swallow, sparrow, pigeon, or magpie," the eagle responded. "I really don't care. Go away." The massive bird picked himself up and turned his back, tugging at the cord that held him prisoner.

Ragtag's curiosity won out over his fear. Seeing that the eagle was incapable of harming him even if he wanted to, the swallow jumped up and hopped about to get a better look.

"You're trapped," he squeaked, careful to keep out of reach of the raptor's free talon.

The eagle turned a withering eye on him. "You're an intelligent little thing, aren't you?"

"I thought you were a cat or some sort of monster, the way you came at me like that. You almost scared me to death!"

The eagle ignored Ragtag and continued to peck at the wood beneath him. Try as he might, he couldn't gain enough leverage to break free.

Ragtag hopped closer. "What are you, anyway?"

"Stupid swallow! Don't you know an eagle when you see one?" The great bird drew himself up. "I'm a bald eagle," he declared haughtily. "The greatest of all who take to the air. Now go away!"

"I've never seen an eagle in the city before," Ragtag said. "Where do you come from?" He suddenly hopped back as a terrifying thought occurred to him. "Are you a scout for the Talon Empire?"

"Talon Empire?" the eagle said. "What are you babbling about?"

"You know!" Ragtag chirped. "The raptors who are about to attack the city."

"Don't be silly."

"Don't lie!"

"Eagles never lie!" the large bird roared, and shook his wings. Ragtag fluttered back and hit the wall.

The eagle lowered his wings. "Eagles never lie," he repeated, his voice a bit calmer. "I'm not familiar with this empire you speak of, but know this, little swallow: Eagles swear allegiance to none but themselves."

"If you're not from the empire," Ragtag said, a bit put out, "where are you from?"

"Far from here."

"From the west?"

"Try again."

"From the east!"

"My, you are quick."

"You flew here from across the harbor?"

"Farther even than that."

As lightning flashed again, Ragtag could see that blood ran from a cut on the eagle's head, staining his feathers.

"You're bleeding!" Ragtag cried, and moved forward, all fear forgotten. "What happened to you?"

"I told you to leave me alone."

"Not until you tell me!" Ragtag said as he continued to hop about the giant bird.

"Stop! You're making me dizzy."

Ragtag stopped and cocked his head to one side. The eagle sighed. "Fine, if you must know, I'm being hunted."

"Hunted by who?"

"Are you really that dense?" the eagle said as he resumed working to free the cord. "There is only one creature who has the ability to hunt an eagle—a human, of course!"

"But why?" Ragtag cried.

"Because they want me to live in a cage. And I'll tell you right now, I'd rather die than go back!"

"I've heard of caged birds before," Ragtag said. "But I always thought those were stories made up to scare fledglings."

The eagle's voice suddenly quavered and grew heavy. "You don't know how lucky you are to be free, little swallow. To feel the wind, to fly where you choose, when you choose."

The eagle pulled at the cord with his talon, struggling to free himself. His efforts were futile; his beak was simply too large. Finally he gave up and turned back to Ragtag.

"Once I was free like you," the eagle said. "Once I roamed the skies far from here. And then, on a horrible day not too long ago, I was captured, ensnared by the humans in their nets. Do you know what it's like to be put in a cage? To never be able to stretch your wings?"

Ragtag didn't answer. He was awed by the pain in the great bird's voice.

"No, I don't believe you do," the eagle continued. "Trust me when I say it's a fate worse than death. So when I saw a chance to escape, I took it."

The eagle roused himself and attacked the floorboard with all his might. He succeeded only in wedging the cord in tighter.

Ragtag took a hesitant step forward. "Maybe I can help you?"

The eagle stared at him with hope. "If you did, I would be forever in your debt!"

"Do you really mean it?" asked Ragtag.

"I give you my word of honor," replied the eagle. "Know this: The promise of a bald eagle is the most sacred promise in the world. If you help me now, I swear I shall come to your aid if ever you need me."

Ragtag thought fast. What if the giant bird was lying? He could rip Ragtag to shreds. But if he was telling the truth, then he would owe his freedom to Ragtag. A shrewd idea was growing in the back of the swallow's mind. If he could get this eagle to help defend the Feathered Alliance from the Talon Empire, he would be considered a hero. He could just imagine Bobtail's and Proud Beak's jealousy.

"Okay, I'm going to trust you," Ragtag said. "Hold still, I'm coming closer."

Ragtag cautiously hopped beneath the giant bird. Burrowing his smaller beak between the beams, he pecked at the cord until it finally gave way. The eagle flapped his wings in relief and gingerly tested his freed talon.

"You have my thanks," said the eagle. "And from this day forward, my friendship. My name is Baldur."

"I'm called Ragtag!"

"Indeed," Baldur said with a hint of amusement. "Well, it's certainly a fitting description."

Ragtag hopped about excitedly. "The Feathered Alliance is having a big meeting right now. All the clan leaders are there.

Will you come back with me? Nobody will believe I made friends with an eagle unless you come!"

"Nothing would please me more," replied Baldur, "but I'm too tired to fly. I must sleep now." The eagle settled himself in a corner and folded his wings.

"Okay," Ragtag said. "I'll bring them here. I can't wait to see their faces when they meet you!"

"I don't suppose you could bring me back some food?"

"What would you like?"

"A freshly killed rabbit would be nice."

The swallow hesitated. "That might be a bit difficult."

"Never mind, then."

Ragtag stopped next to a window and glanced back at his new friend. "Promise me you won't leave before I return?"

"I promise. I'll be here," Baldur said, then yawned sleepily and closed his eyes.

Ragtag took to the air, despite the pelting rain and howling wind, and headed back toward Copley Square.

Hoogol

The Council Meeting

R agtag tried his best to ignore the lightning and thunder. He squinted into the pounding rain, trying to keep on course as the wind buffeted him without mercy.

The swallow couldn't wait to tell the clan leaders of his discovery. Thoughts of glory were already spinning through his head. He could just imagine their reaction when they learned that he had discovered a weapon that might defeat the Talon Empire. He could already hear their cheers. No doubt he would be presented with some sort of medal. But the greatest delight of all would be watching Bobtail's and Proud Beak's reactions. No longer would his older brother be the center of attention, and no longer would he himself be the object of the cardinal's endless jokes.

Ragtag spread his wings as the wind picked him up and carried him across Copley Square. The Old South Church, his first home, suddenly appeared out of the darkness, and it took all his strength to keep from overshooting the belfry ledge. He landed rather ungracefully, shook himself off, and hopped inside.

The belfry tower had open-air windows in each of its four walls. As the wind entered the chamber, it caused the large bell to whistle and groan as if it were alive. Ragtag had never cared much for the belfry. Once a week, the bell rang so loudly it could be heard clear across the river. The birds had learned that when crowds of humans gathered at the church, it was only a matter of time before the noise began. Those birds who didn't depart immediately risked being knocked senseless by the clamor. Having grown up in the church, Ragtag was used to it, but the noise still gave him a headache.

He moved forward, surprised at the number of birds in attendance. Gulls, pigeons, cardinals, chickadees, finches, blue jays, robins, sparrows, starlings, and swifts were all talking at once.

"Excuse me, coming through," Ragtag said as he tried to force his way through the sea of brightly colored plumage. A tail suddenly whacked him in the face.

"Sorry, Ragtag," said a female mockingbird named Kittiwook as she tried to round up two of her children.

"That's okay, Kittiwook. Has the meeting started yet?"

"No. Hoogol is late tonight."

Ragtag continued on, crossing in front of a flock of pigeons who were nervously cooing around their leader, a plump female named Bragi. Ragtag kept as quiet as possible as he made his way past, hoping he could get through them without being noticed.

"Ragtag!" Bragi cried. Ragtag's spirits sank as she waddled over to him. Pigeons were notorious talkers. Once they cornered you, it was almost impossible to escape.

"Oh, my poor, dear Ragtag," Bragi continued, her feathers quivering. "It's hopeless. We're all doomed."

The pigeons huddled around her chanted in unison. "Doomed! Doomed!"

Ragtag sighed. Pigeons were hardly the bravest of souls. "Bragi, I'm looking for Bobtail and my mother," he said impatiently. "Have you seen them?"

"Blue Feather's around here somewhere," Bragi clucked. "Heaven knows it's a wonder anyone can find anybody in this crowd. There are simply too many birds here. And where, oh where is Hoogol? I really think it's rather impolite that he calls a meeting and then doesn't even bother showing up. But that's the problem with owls. No sense of decency. They are raptors, you know. Horrible beasts."

Bragi shuddered, and her flock did the same. "Heaven help us," she continued. "What would my poor mother say if she knew that a bird of prey was leading the Feathered Alliance? We're doomed, I tell you."

"Doomed! Doomed!" repeated her flock.

As Bragi's attention was diverted by her followers, Ragtag saw an opening in the crowd and ducked away. He was thankful for the escape. One could easily spend all night listening to pigeons and never get a word in edgewise.

Ragtag continued to push his way through the crowd. He had never seen so many birds in one place. Usually the council meetings were poorly attended. Tonight, it seemed as if every bird in the Feathered Alliance had turned up.

A hush fell over the belfry as a shadow swooped silently overhead. Ragtag felt a chill go down his spine, and he took a timid step back. Even though he had known Hoogol all his life, he was still unnerved by how quietly the great horned owl could fly.

Hoogol landed in an open space near the center of the belfry and shook the rain off his wings. His head swiveled from side to side, his large yellow eyes scanning the crowd.

Proud Beak hopped forward and whispered something to him. Hoogol was so much larger that he had to bend his head to hear the cardinal speak. Ragtag watched as Hoogol's eyes blinked once, then twice. The swallow was always awestruck in the presence of the owl.

Hoogol wasn't city born. Many years ago, when he was still young, he had arrived from the west, wounded and seeking help. A seagull named Heimdall took him in. At that time, the various clans of the city were still at odds, and wars frequently broke out. With the help of Heimdall, Hoogol forged a peace treaty that led to the foundation of the Feathered Alliance. It was Hoogol who had united the clans and brought peace to the birds of the city, and as a result, he was revered and treated with the utmost respect by all.

The owl nodded to Proud Beak. The cardinal hopped forward and shook his wings for silence.

"Quiet, everyone," Proud Beak ordered. "Hoogol is about to speak."

The birds settled down. Ragtag suddenly spotted Bobtail and Blue Feather on the far side of the belfry and jostled his way through a crowd of young starlings to reach them.

"Well, well," whispered Bobtail as he caught sight of his brother. "Look who decided to show up after all."

"Bobtail! Mom!" Ragtag exclaimed. "You won't believe what I found."

Proud Beak zeroed in on the young swallow, a look of disdain on his face. "Ragtag, be quiet!"

"But this is important!" Ragtag protested.

"I don't care. Hoogol is about to speak."

"But—"

"Be quiet or leave!" Proud Beak waited to see if Ragtag would interrupt him again. Ragtag tapped his foot in anger and indignation but kept quiet. When Proud Beak was convinced Ragtag had finished, he glanced disapprovingly at Blue Feather. "Quite a handful you've got there."

"Sorry, Proud Beak," Blue Feather said, giving Ragtag a stern look.

The cardinal turned and bowed low before Hoogol. "I apologize for the interruption. You may begin."

The owl stared at Ragtag curiously, then cleared his throat. The birds leaned forward and held their breath.

For a long moment, Hoogol remained silent. His eyes neither blinked nor moved. A few of the birds restlessly tapped their claws on the belfry's floor. It was a well-known fact that the old owl had a tendency to fall asleep with his eyes open. Sometimes council meetings went on for hours without anyone being the wiser.

But this time, Hoogol wasn't sleeping. The great horned owl was carefully measuring his thoughts. When he finally did speak, the crowd hung on his every word.

"For many years," Hoogol began in a booming voice, "the rooftops of our great city have been governed by the

Feathered Alliance. Under our guidance, the clans have lived in harmony. With the exception of the treacherous crows, we have been at peace."

At the mention of the crows, Ragtag stole a glance at Tattler, who was standing beside Hoogol. He watched as the sparrow tensed. Ragtag knew Tattler hated the very mention of the clan. When she was a fledgling, her family had been attacked by a marauding band of crows. Her parents had tried to defend their nest but were outnumbered, and they had been killed along with her brothers. Tattler herself wouldn't have survived if it hadn't been for Hoogol. The owl had been flying overhead at the time and had quickly gone to her aid, giving her to Blue Feather to nurse back to health. She had stayed close to the family of swallows and was like an older sister to Ragtag.

"But now," Hoogol continued, drawing Ragtag's attention back to him, "I'm sad to say that we face a threat far greater than the crows. I fear our way of life is about to end."

A murmur of fear ran through the crowd. Bobtail and Blue Feather exchanged nervous glances, while Ragtag continued to tap his foot. He had to use all his self-control not to jump forward and blurt out his news—that the Feathered Alliance could be saved with Baldur's help.

"I have called this meeting to tell you what some of you already know," Hoogol said, his voice heavy. "A great darkness looms over us. The Talon Empire is advancing upon us from the west. Already they control the lands beyond the river. Only our city remains as a stronghold for those who desire peace.

"Know this: They are relentless, and are driven by an emperor who cannot be reasoned with. They will not stop until every bird in our city has been enslaved and the Feathered Alliance brought to its knees. My friends, I fear it's only a matter of time until we're attacked."

A wave of panic swept through the belfry, and everyone began talking at once. As usual, the pigeons made the biggest ruckus. "Who will defend us?" one of them cried.

"We're not warriors," said another. "We're just pigeons!"

"Please, everyone remain calm," Proud Beak yelled as he hopped about in front of Hoogol.

A starling named Gini fluttered into the air. "Who is this emperor, and what does he want?"

Hoogol's head swiveled to look at her. "His name is Bergelmir."

A hush fell over the birds. Even Ragtag found himself trembling.

"You say his name as if you know him," Gini ventured.

"I know of him," Hoogol replied.

Everyone pricked up their ears. They all knew the story Hoogol told of his origins. But nobody quite believed it. For one thing, Hoogol had never shown any interest in finding his lost relatives. For another, he never talked about them. A lot of birds thought Hoogol had made up the story to hide the truth, whatever that was. But nobody dared question him further. It wasn't wise to ask prying questions of a great horned owl.

"Before I came to this city," Hoogol offered when the silence had grown uncomfortable, "I had heard stories of the

Talon Empire. I had always assumed that they were just legends and myths. Now I realize they were true.

"Bergelmir is an osprey," Hoogol continued, "one of the deadliest of raptors. He is consumed by an unquenchable lust for power. We will not be able to negotiate with him. He is, I believe, one of the most dangerous creatures alive."

"What do they want?" Kittiwook asked as she tried to calm her terrified children.

"It's quite simple," Hoogol replied. "They want to conquer us, to force us to do their bidding."

"But why now?" Blue Feather asked. "The city has been left undisturbed for years."

Proud Beak hopped forward. "Our scouts have informed us that the humans and their machines have been cutting down the great woods to the west that were home to the empire. That is why they are now advancing."

The birds began to twitter in despair.

"Stupid humans!" a chickadee cried out.

"We're doomed," Bragi muttered.

"Doomed! Doomed!" The pigeons' chant echoed through the belfry.

"What chance do we have?" Gini said. "We're no match against raptors! Do we just give up?"

"I have something to say!" Ragtag yelled as he hopped forward. He couldn't keep quiet anymore. "I know a way to—"

"Be quiet, Ragtag!" Proud Beak roared, then turned back to Gini. "The Feathered Alliance will never give up. We'll find a way to rout these birds and send Bergelmir back where he came from!"

"I'd like to hear from Tattler," Kittiwook said. "She's the leader of the Winged Regiment."

"Yes, yes," Bragi agreed. "It's their job to protect us!"

"Protect us! Protect us!" the pigeons clucked.

Tattler moved forward and cleared her throat. "We have about two hundred sparrows stationed by the river in case the raptors try to cross."

"Will you be able to stop them?"

Tattler looked uncomfortable. "As you all know, the Winged Regiment was formed to protect the clans from crows, ravens, and other enemies. We greatly outnumber the raptors, but we're no match against their larger size and strength. If they try to cross the river, the best we can do is slow them down."

The belfry echoed with the whispers of anxious birds.

"We're doomed!" Bragi wailed, and hid her head beneath her wings.

Ragtag was beginning to lose patience. He fluttered into the air. "I have something to say!"

But nobody listened to him. Hoogol and Proud Beak tried to calm the pigeons as fear and panic spread among the rest of the crowd. Ragtag called for their attention, but his voice was drowned out by the screeches, chirps, and squawks of the other birds.

Suddenly there was a flash of dark feathers. Everyone froze as a jet-black crow landed in the belfry.

Loki

The Treachery of the Crows

L oki!" Hoogol thundered.

Instantly Tattler and two of her lieutenants sprang forward, slamming into the startled crow and knocking him off balance. The other birds gasped at the viciousness of the attack.

"Tattler, leave him alone!" Hoogol said. "Nobody is to touch him unless I say so!"

Tattler and the other sparrows disengaged themselves and fluttered back. She was trembling with anger. Everyone knew of her hatred for the crows. It was all she could do to obey Hoogol's order.

All eyes turned to Loki. Ragtag watched with fascination as the crow leader slowly climbed to his feet. The crows were hated and feared. Hoogol had banned Loki from entering the belfry under penalty of death. Whatever had brought him here must be of dire importance.

Loki's feathers were ripped and stuck out in all directions, but he showed no sign of pain. He shook out his wings and folded them behind his back.

"So this is how you treat guests?" Loki cackled at Hoogol.

"You are not our guest," Hoogol replied, his voice stern. "Your kind is not welcome here."

Proud Beak hopped forward. "You have some nerve! You crows are nothing but liars and thieves who attack our families and steal our eggs from our nests."

"The crows are murderers!" Tattler yelled.

"We have a right to survive," Loki said, a hint of annoyance in his voice.

"The crows were given a chance to join the Feathered Alliance," Hoogol replied. "You shunned our offer. Have you forgotten?"

"Or perhaps you've now come seeking protection from the Talon Empire?" Proud Beak added with a sneer.

"The crows need help from no one, least of all your useless alliance," Loki spat at the cardinal.

Proud Beak and Tattler jumped forward. They looked ready to finish him off once and for all.

"Hold, Tattler," said Hoogol. The great horned owl towered over Loki. "What do you want? Why are you here?"

"I've come to deliver a message."

"A message from whom?"

"Why, from Bergelmir, of course."

Tattler and the sparrows would have torn the crow apart then and there if not for Hoogol's stern glance.

"Traitor!" Proud Beak yelled. "You would join forces with the likes of the Talon Empire?"

"Why not?" Loki laughed. "I'm practical. The Feathered

Alliance is weak. In a few days, it will no longer exist. I prefer to cast my lot with the strong. That's the nature of survival."

The crowd erupted in anger. Ragtag watched Hoogol, whose giant eyes stared at the crow. Curiously, he seemed more sad than angry.

Hoogol waited until the noise had died down, then addressed the crow leader once more. "I don't know what agreement you've made with Bergelmir, Loki, or what he's promised you in return for your treachery. But I fear you've made a great mistake. The emperor cannot be trusted. If the birds of prey overrun the city, do you really believe the crows will remain untouched?"

"I don't care what you think," Loki replied. "You're old, Hoogol. You've grown weak, and your mind is feeble. A great storm is about to sweep over this city, a storm that only the strong will survive. I doubt you will be among them."

For the first time since the crow had entered the belfry, a flicker of anger showed on Hoogol's face. The great horned owl drew himself up to his full height, his feathers bristling. "You came here to deliver a message, Loki," he said. "Deliver it and then depart, before I change my mind and have you ripped to shreds."

Loki faced the clan leaders. "My message is this," he said in a loud voice. "If the Feathered Alliance surrenders now, without a fight, the emperor will see to it that the clans come to no harm. However, if you resist, if you continue to follow this owl . . . you will all be destroyed."

The crowd cried out, forcing Hoogol to flap his wings for silence.

"You have heard Loki's message," Hoogol said. "Any of you who wish to leave the Feathered Alliance, now is the time. Any of you who wish to go with Loki and bow before Bergelmir, I will not reproach you or think less of you for doing so. Indeed, if Loki is correct in his thinking, it may be your only chance for survival. Make your decision."

A hush fell over the belfry. Not a single bird moved. Proud Beak and Tattler hopped forward and closed ranks behind the owl. Hoogol swiveled his massive head, his eyes burning into the crow's.

"There is your answer, Loki. You have delivered your message. Now I have a message for you to take back to Bergelmir. Tell him the Feathered Alliance will never surrender, and that the empire will be fought with every last feather and claw."

"So be it," Loki said. He took to the air and vanished into the rain.

Tattler instinctively spread her wings to give chase.

"Let him go," Hoogol said. "I thought better of you, Tattler. You attacked without provocation and without my order."

The sparrow was crestfallen. "You're right, Hoogol. I'm sorry."

"You should not have let him leave," Proud Beak said. "Loki knows the city as well as any of us. If he's joined with the empire, that knowledge could prove deadly."

"What would you have me do?" Hoogol asked. "Kill him in cold blood?"

"Yes," Proud Beak replied without hesitation.

"If I did so, I fear there would not be much difference between Bergelmir and me."

"I understand what you're saying," the cardinal replied, unable to keep the irritation out of his voice. "But your sense of honor may have cost us greatly. The life of one crow is worthless."

"No life is worthless," Hoogol responded. "All life has potential. Even Loki's. I do not believe he's evil, only misguided."

"Misguided or not, Loki's right," Gini cried from the rear of the belfry. "We can't stop the empire!"

"Our lives are over," Bragi chimed in. "We can't fight them. We're doomed!"

"Doomed! Doomed!" the pigeons cooed.

Worried parents searched the crowd for their children. Others cried out to Hoogol, asking him for guidance and pleading with him to save them. Hoogol didn't answer. The owl's head was lowered, and he seemed tired.

"Come on—think, everyone!" Bobtail yelled. "We have to come up with a plan."

"Plan?" Kittiwook repeated from where she stood with the other mockingbirds. "What do we need to plan? Our funerals?"

"We have to defend the city!" Blue Feather announced.

"But how?" Bragi protested. "It's hopeless!"

"Bragi's right," Gini chirped. "There's not a bird here who can go head-to-head with a falcon or a hawk."

"Hoogol can!" Proud Beak said.

Hoogol slowly shook his head. "At one time, perhaps, when I was younger. But now, I'm afraid Loki's right. I've grown too old and weak to make much of a difference."

Ragtag was growing increasingly impatient. He hopped up and down at the back of the belfry. "I've got something to say!"

Nobody paid him any attention.

"Then we have no choice!" Blue Feather said. "We have to abandon the city."

"You mean run away!" Proud Beak roared.

"What's wrong with that?" Bragi asked.

"Yes, yes!" another pigeon added. "Run and live!"

"You can run," Tattler said. "But I'm staying. This city is my home."

"I'm staying, too!" Bobtail declared, not wanting to be seen as less brave than anyone else.

"I've got something to say!" Ragtag yelled.

"Nobody cares what you've got to say," Bobtail retorted.

"Even if we did leave the city," Proud Beak said, ignoring Ragtag, "where would we go?"

"That's right," chirped Tattler's second-in-command, a male sparrow named Headstrong. "We would spend the rest of our days looking over our shoulders. It would be only a matter of time until the empire found us."

Everyone started talking and arguing at once.

"I know how we can fight the empire!" Ragtag yelled. Losing patience, he fluttered into the air and flew headfirst into the giant bell. A *bong* rolled out, and the swallow dropped with a squawk in front of Hoogol. At last the room was quiet. The crowd stared with disapproval at the excited bird.

"*Hmmph!*" Proud Beak said. "I think Ragtag has something to say."

"Let's hear from Ragtag," Kittiwook chimed in.

"Yes, tell us what you think," Bobtail said. "I'm sure you've given it a great deal of thought."

Ragtag jumped to his feet. He shook out his wings, then turned to face the crowd. "There is one type of bird who could fight Bergelmir and win."

"Who?" Proud Beak asked.

"An eagle!" he proudly declared.

Tattler

Banished

Stunned silence filled the belfry. Ragtag looked around, expecting to be cheered. He couldn't hide his disappointment when the other birds began screeching with laughter. Even Hoogol seemed amused.

"Ragtag," said the great horned owl, "everyone knows there are no eagles in the city."

"That's not true! I found one today. His name is Baldur."

"What are you babbling about?" Proud Beak snapped. "Enough of this!"

"No, it's true!" Ragtag said, hopping in front of the owl. "He was trapped in that abandoned factory near the bridge. I helped free him, and he promised in return to come to my aid if I ever asked. Don't you see? We can get him to fight the emperor for us. No bird can stand up to an eagle, not even an osprey. Not even Bergelmir!"

Ragtag expected to be showered with gratitude and praise. Instead, the birds were downright dismissive, even insulting.

"Heaven help us," Gini chirped. "Who let this child into the meeting?"

"It's clear he made up this story just to get attention," Proud Beak announced.

"I did not!"

"Throw him out of the belfry!" a robin chimed from the back of the crowd.

"Yes, yes, out he goes," Bragi clucked.

The crowd murmured its agreement. Ragtag looked to his mother for support, but Blue Feather averted her eyes. He turned desperately to Hoogol, who was watching him carefully.

"Baldur is real!" Ragtag cried. "I'm telling the truth."

Hoogol didn't reply, and Ragtag wondered if the old owl had once again fallen asleep with his eyes open.

"If you really did help an eagle, where is he?" Proud Beak asked. "Or is this Baldur an imaginary friend of yours?"

"Maybe he's an invisible eagle," Bobtail added. Everyone except Blue Feather, Hoogol, and Tattler joined in the laughter.

"He was injured!" Ragtag protested. "He's still there in that old building. He promised he would wait for my return."

"What if it's a trap?" a chickadee chirped. "What if this eagle's a scout for the Talon Empire?"

"Unlikely," Tattler said. "Eagles serve only themselves. They never associate with other birds of prey, or bow before the likes of Bergelmir."

"It couldn't have been an eagle," Proud Beak said. "An eagle has never been seen in the city before. You expect me to believe Ragtag just happened to find one? And that this eagle is now in his debt and willing to help us? Bah! I'm telling you, he's making it up."

Ragtag hopped in front of Hoogol, a pleading look in his eyes. "I swear I'm telling the truth. If you don't believe me, I'll take you to him. You can see him yourself!"

Everyone fell silent, curious to see what Hoogol would say. The great horned owl stared at Ragtag, who held his ground and refused to look away.

"Ragtag," Hoogol finally said. "We're here tonight to discuss a very serious matter. This is neither the time nor the place for pranks. Do you understand what I'm saying?"

"I understand."

"And do you also understand," Hoogol continued, his voice once again stern, "that if the council follows you to this attic and there is no eagle, you will be banished?"

"I'm telling the truth!"

Hoogol gazed at him with unblinking eyes, then said, "Very well. Lead the way and we will follow."

"What?" Proud Beak gasped. "You can't be serious."

"I've never been more so."

"But it's cold and raining outside," Bobtail protested.

"Then I advise you to stay here," Hoogol replied. "However, if Ragtag is telling the truth, then I wish to speak to this eagle. Lead the way, Ragtag."

Ragtag took to the air and left the belfry with Hoogol on his tail. One by one, the rest of the clan leaders took flight and followed, until only Bobtail was left. He cursed and grumbled to himself; then he, too, spread his wings and hurried to catch up.

The storm continued to rage over the city. Most of the humans had taken shelter indoors. If any had been daring enough to brave the elements, they would have seen a strange sight: dozens of types of birds flying in formation, being buffeted by the wind as they headed north over Copley Square.

Ragtag led the way through the pounding rain. He had been stung by the criticism in the belfry and was determined to prove himself. He would show them he wasn't a liar. He wanted nothing more than to listen to Bobtail's and Proud Beak's apologies.

A flash of lightning lit the streets below. Ragtag swooped down toward the abandoned factory and fluttered through the broken window. The attic was exactly as he had left it. Hoogol landed next to him and shook the water off his wings. One by one, the other birds arrived. All of them were cold, wet, and shivering.

"Baldur?" Ragtag said loudly. There was no answer. He hopped over to the crates. "Baldur, it's me, Ragtag!"

Ragtag waited for a reply. His only answer was the roar of the rain.

"Well?" Proud Beak asked. "Where's this eagle of yours?"

Dozens of eyes stared at Ragtag. He hopped into the shadows, hoping to find Baldur asleep in a corner. He hopped left, then right; forward, then back. There was no sign of the eagle.

"Ragtag?" Blue Feather asked, a touch of kindness in her voice.

"He was right here!" Ragtag squeaked, fluttering across the empty floor.

"I told you," Bobtail said with an exaggerated sigh. "My little brother has a somewhat overactive imagination."

Ragtag ignored him and desperately flew back and forth as the others watched. "Baldur, where are you?"

"Maybe you just imagined it was an eagle," Blue Feather gently suggested. "The lightning could have played tricks on your eyes. Some of these crates could have cast shadows that looked like an eagle. . . ."

"I can tell the difference between a shadow and an eagle," Ragtag said with more anger than he intended. "He was here! I talked to him!"

"I suggest we head back to the belfry," Proud Beak said to Hoogol.

"Look!" Ragtag exclaimed. He flew over to the broken floorboard. "This is where he was trapped! See?"

"All I see," said Gini, "is a jagged piece of wood."

"He was bleeding! You can see the stain."

The other birds crowded around. In the darkness, it was impossible to see much of anything.

"You've got to believe me," Ragtag wailed as he hopped about. "Baldur is real! He promised he would stay here until I came back."

The swallow knew the clan leaders were looking at him with disapproval. He could hear them whispering behind his back, but he didn't care. What bothered him most was that Hoogol hadn't said a word.

"Baldur!" Ragtag yelled. "Where are you?"

Proud Beak hopped forward. "Enough! We don't have time for these foolish games. All of us are in danger, and you're making up stories."

"I'm not making up stories. Baldur?"

"Quiet, Ragtag," Proud Beak said.

"You be quiet!" Ragtag retorted.

"What did you just say?" the cardinal asked in shock.

"This is a disgrace!" Gini yelled. "Hoogol, are you listening? Are you going to let this youngster talk so rudely to his elders?"

Hoogol didn't reply. He just watched as Ragtag flapped around the attic, growing more and more frantic.

"Ragtag, enough!" Bobtail yelled. "It's clear to everyone that you're a liar. I'm ashamed that you're my brother!"

This was too much for Ragtag to handle. He plowed into Bobtail. Feathers flew as the two birds snapped angrily at each other.

Proud Beak leaped into the fray. The cardinal jumped on top of Ragtag, pinning him down while Bobtail scrambled away.

"He's gone mad!" Bobtail gasped.

"This is too much, Hoogol," Proud Beak said. "We're wasting time."

Hoogol motioned for him to release Ragtag. Proud Beak hopped back, but Ragtag didn't get up. He lay motionless on the floor.

"You're right, Proud Beak," Hoogol said with sadness. "Enough is enough." The great horned owl swiveled his head so that he was facing the young swallow. "Ragtag, there is no eagle and there never was. I trusted you and you lied to me. You lied to us all and wasted precious time. You have cost us dearly tonight, and will be punished accordingly. From this moment forward, consider yourself banished. I'm sorry, but you brought this on yourself."

Hoogol spread his wings and departed. The others followed until only Bobtail and Blue Feather remained.

"Ragtag . . ." Blue Feather began.

"Go away!" Ragtag shouted.

Bobtail whispered to his mother that it would be best if they left him alone. The two birds flew off together through the broken window as Ragtag continued to lie on the floor.

Tattler suddenly appeared and examined the bloodstain with interest.

"Go ahead," Ragtag whispered as he caught sight of her. "Call me a liar, too."

"I've known you since you were born, Ragtag," Tattler said. "You may be many things, but you're not a liar. I believe you. I'm just curious about what happened to your eagle."

The sparrow hopped over and pecked at the broken beam as Ragtag crawled to his feet. "He lied to me. He flew away when he said he would stay."

"Perhaps," Tattler said as she looked around. "I'm not an expert, but from what I know of eagles, I don't think they lie."

"It doesn't matter," Ragtag cried. "I've been banished from the alliance. Well, if they don't want me around, that's fine. I'll go. I'll run away. They'll never see me again!"

"Ragtag, wait—"

It was too late. The swallow had taken flight, and bolted out the window before Tattler could stop him.

Ragtag spread his wings and let the wind carry him through the driving rain. As he glided away from the factory, he didn't bother to look down. If he had, he might have seen the humans with their lights, loading a caged and tranquilized eagle into the back of a van.

Bergelmir

The Birds of Prey

T he first light of dawn found hundreds of sparrows perched in the trees along the southern banks of the Charles River, their eyes trained for any sign of movement from the opposite shore.

Tattler gazed out from her post high atop an oak tree. She couldn't help shivering. Although she couldn't see them, she knew from her scouts that the enemy was hidden on the far side of the river. The sparrow glanced at the other members of the Winged Regiment in the trees around her. All of them had families, and even though Hoogol had ordered the evacuation of the clans to the far side of the city, they were still worried.

Tattler thought of Ragtag, Bobtail, and Blue Feather. They were the only family she had, and she was determined to protect them. Her claws tightened on the branch beneath her, and she forced herself to focus on the job at hand. The Winged Regiment was now more than two hundred sparrows strong. She was proud that they had managed to pull together their reserves. It was her hope that what the sparrows lacked in size they would make up for in sheer numbers.

"There's no sign of movement," Headstrong reported as he landed next to her.

"They're there," Tattler told her second-in-command. "They're hiding."

"How can you be so sure?"

"Look at the far side of the river. On a typical morning, you'd expect to see hundreds of birds foraging for food."

"And today, there's not a wing in the sky," Headstrong muttered. Then he flew off to inspect the rest of the troops.

Tattler's thoughts drifted back to the events of the previous night. She had tried to chase Ragtag, but he had vanished in the storm. Even if she had managed to catch up with him, she wouldn't have known what to say. Ragtag wasn't a liar, but even Tattler couldn't help doubting his story about the eagle. It was just too fantastic. Perhaps Blue Feather had been right. What with the excitement of the storm and the council meeting, maybe he had imagined it.

A sudden commotion in the trees pulled Tattler back to the present. Loki darted from the underbrush, chased by a pair of female sparrows. The crow was making a run for the opposite shore.

"Traitor!" Tattler yelled, and launched herself into the air along with a dozen others. The sparrows quickly closed the gap. As they skimmed over the water, Tattler's spirits soared. There was no way the crow could outfly them. They would bring Loki down before he had a chance to betray them.

"Watch out!" Headstrong cried. A shadow fell on them

from above. Tattler's blood ran cold as a pair of red-tailed hawks dove out of the sky. They cut the sparrows off, talons raking the air.

"Fall back!" Tattler ordered. Her spirits crumbled as the sparrows darted away in all directions.

Loki laughed gleefully while the hawks escorted him safely across the river. Dozens of raptors were hidden amid the trees lining the far bank. As he approached, he spotted kestrels, merlins, and harriers of every shape and size.

For a brief moment, Loki wavered. Was he doing the right thing? He was about to hand over the entire city to the empire. The crow glanced at his escorts as they continued inland. The larger of the two hawks was named Gunlad. He was the leader of the hawks and Bergelmir's third-in-command. It was Gunlad who had been the go-between when Loki had first approached the raptors.

The crows had a network of spies that stretched far beyond the boundaries of the city, so it had come as no surprise when Loki learned that the empire was advancing. At first he thought of declaring a truce with the Feathered Alliance and combining its might with the crows' in order to repel the birds of prey. But Loki had quickly realized that such a move would delay the inevitable only by a few days at best. So under the cover of night, he had slipped across the river and offered the emperor a deal.

Gunlad and his partner tightened their formation, forcing Loki to climb toward the top of a large building. Loki quickly shook off his hesitation. There was no turning back now. Besides, the crow reasoned, his actions would save lives. A full-scale war between the Feathered Alliance and the Talon Empire would result in utter devastation and needless deaths. At least this way, the other clans might be enslaved, but they would still be alive.

And the crows would be free. That was Loki's goal, and he reminded himself not to forget it.

The hawks spread their wings and glided to a landing atop a tar-covered roof. Gunlad quickly ushered Loki to a corner that was protected by the overhanging branches of a tree.

Beneath it sat the emperor, Bergelmir. The osprey's feathers were peppered white with age. A pair of beady eyes stared out over a hooked beak that seemed to be carved in a perpetual sneer.

As Loki watched, Bergelmir ripped apart a fish with his talons and swallowed the chunks whole. The crow felt queasy and kept his eyes averted until the emperor had finished his meal.

"M'lord," Loki said, bowing low.

Before Bergelmir could reply, a voice rang out from behind the crow. "Well, well. If it isn't the traitor come to practice his skills."

The hawks laughed as Loki whirled to face a massive peregrine falcon. The crow swallowed nervously and took a step back. Surt was the heir to Bergelmir's throne. His white face had heavy black stripes that looked like sideburns, and there were brown spots and bars on his chest.

Loki didn't like Surt. Bergelmir had a shrewd quality that the crow could appreciate, but Surt was concerned only with power. The peregrine falcon towered over the other raptors. His muscles rippled when he moved, and his razor-sharp talons flashed in the sun.

"Well?" the falcon asked again as his hooked beak moved menacingly closer.

"Y-yes," stammered Loki. "I mean, no. I mean—"

"You mean what?" Surt demanded.

Loki glanced nervously at Bergelmir. "I gave Hoogol your message, as instructed."

Bergelmir stirred at the mention of the owl's name. When he spoke, it was with a rasp that reflected his great age. "And how did my old friend reply?"

Loki hesitated, realizing that the emperor might order Surt to rip him apart when he heard the news.

"Well?" Bergelmir demanded.

"He respectfully declined your generous offer," Loki said, then hastily added, "He's a senile old fool."

"Perhaps," Bergelmir replied. "But just because he refuses me, doesn't make him a fool. And just because he's old, doesn't make him senile."

Loki gulped nervously. Surt was standing behind him, slowing running his beak through the crow's feathers, much to Loki's discomfort.

"Tell me, crow," Bergelmir said with a hint of boredom. "Are you ready to fulfill your part of our bargain?"

Loki hopped away from Surt. "As long as we're in agreement," the crow replied. "I'll betray the Feathered Alliance on one condition—that the crows in the city remain free."

"Then it's agreed. Surt, I will talk with you alone."

The falcon and the osprey left the crow and flew to the far side of the roof. Surt took a nervous step back as he gazed down at the moving cars.

"You don't like the city," Bergelmir said.

"I don't trust it," Surt replied. "It's full of strange sounds and even stranger creatures."

"It's full of weak creatures, creatures who have grown soft and complacent away from the wild."

"What about them?" Surt indicated the humans below.

"They are ignorant of us," Bergelmir replied. "I have watched them for a long time. They don't care about our world."

"I hate them," Surt said.

"As do I," Bergelmir agreed.

The osprey and the falcon fell silent as they thought about their old home. A few months earlier, the humans had come with their loud machines, brightly colored bulldozers and whining saws that cut down the trees where the raptors dwelled. With the woods vanishing and their food supply dwindling, the birds of prey had been forced to seek a new home.

Surt glanced at Loki. "You trust this crow?"

"No," Bergelmir said. "But he will do what needs to be done to ensure the survival of his clan. That is all that matters."

The emperor turned his attention back to the river. "Take Gunlad and five of his best hawks. We will wait for your signal by the river. I trust you won't disappoint me."

Surt bowed low before his emperor. "The Feathered Alliance will be crushed."

Bergelmir ordered his bodyguards to follow him and took to the air. Surt watched as the raptors headed south toward the river; then he made his way back to Loki.

"Know this now that the emperor's away," Surt snarled. "Bergelmir trusts you far more than I do. If you betray us . . ." The peregrine falcon raked his talons against the roof.

Loki's eyes bulged, and he had to force himself not to bolt in fear. "I swear I will not!"

"You have a way of leading us behind enemy lines?"

"Yes!" Loki said, and hopped forward, eager to get on the falcon's good side. "The Winged Regiment are massed along the river. They think nobody can pass them without being noticed." A hint of amusement appeared on Loki's face. "They underestimate the intelligence of us crows."

"Stop babbling about your intelligence and show me!" Surt snapped, then followed Loki as the crow rose toward the sky.

A miserable-looking swallow sat on a dock next to the harbor. Ragtag stared at the water, wondering what had happened. He felt as if he had flown headfirst into a skyscraper. One minute he was about to be hailed as a hero for saving the Feathered Alliance, the next he was banished and an outcast.

What could have happened? He had seen the injured eagle with his own eyes. He had talked to Baldur and set him free. The previous night seemed strangely distant, as if it had been nothing but a dream.

Ragtag shook his head. It hadn't been a dream. Baldur was real and had betrayed him. He had promised to stay in the attic until Ragtag returned. But it seemed that once freed, Baldur hadn't cared about keeping his word.

"So much for the honor of eagles," Ragtag muttered. He was angry at Baldur for making him look like a fool. And he was angry at Hoogol and the clan leaders for not believing him in the first place. It wasn't fair! He had tried to help the Feathered Alliance and had been punished in return.

Ragtag watched the boats bobbing on the waves. The waterfront had always been one of his favorite places. He liked to watch the ships and daydream about the strange and exotic lands they visited.

Maybe I should stow away on one of them, Ragtag thought. That would teach the clan leaders. For the rest of their lives, they'd wonder what had happened to him. He could just imagine Blue Feather blaming Bobtail for provoking him to run away. Not to mention the guilt Hoogol would feel for banishing him in the first place.

"That's what I'm going to do," Ragtag said aloud, trying to convince himself of his own determination. "I'm going to run away!" He spread his wings and flew out over the harbor.

Now that he had made up his mind, he felt better. It was a beautiful morning. The sun was shining and there wasn't a cloud in the sky. Ahead of him lay nothing but the vast ocean and the promise of new adventures.

"Goodbye, Bobtail, Proud Beak, Hoogol, and the rest of you!" Ragtag yelled as he landed atop a ship heading out to sea. He suddenly felt a pang of regret. "Goodbye, Mom," he added with less enthusiasm.

The swallow looked behind him. The city was growing smaller in the distance. Goodbye to Copley Square, Ragtag thought. Never again would he wake up in the trees lining the plaza, stretch lazily as the sun reflected off the skyscrapers, or flutter down to the bushes below to forage for berries. Goodbye to the changing of the seasons, when the trees in the square would turn a rainbow of color and he would happily play in the leaves that the wind gathered behind the Old South Church.

The ship rolled under him as it reached deeper waters. Ragtag fluttered his wings to keep his balance. The ocean suddenly seemed cold and unwelcoming. He glanced back at the receding city and remembered Tattler's words from the previous night. *You can run, but I'm staying,* she'd said. *This city is my home.*

A lump rose in Ragtag's throat. It was his home, too. He spread his wings and flew back to the docks. Landing on a pier, he watched sheepishly as the ship grew smaller and smaller until it finally vanished over the horizon.

I'm such a loser, he thought. I don't even have the courage to run away. He let out a long sigh, wondering what else could possibly go wrong. The answer came when he was splattered by something white from above.

"Sorry," came the distant cry of a pigeon.

Blue Feather

The Invasion of Boston

L oki flew east, followed by Surt and the other raptors. Now that he was actually carrying out his plan, the crow felt a pang of regret. He quickly shook himself. This is a matter of survival, he thought. Besides, he had given Hoogol and the Feathered Alliance a chance to surrender and they had mocked him.

"Why are we flying away from the river?" Surt snapped.

"If you want to cross the river without alerting the Winged Regiment," Loki replied, "there's only one way to do it."

The crow suddenly found what he was looking for and dropped from the sky. The raptors joined him on the sidewalk and watched as he hopped forward and peered through a steel grate in the side of a building. A section of the bars had long ago rusted away, leaving just enough space for them to slip through. Beneath them lay nothing but darkness.

"A hole in a wall?" Gunlad asked suspiciously.

"I'm warning you," Surt said, "if this is some sort of trick—"

"It's no trick," Loki assured them. "However, if you're afraid . . ."

"Lead the way!" the falcon ordered.

Loki hunched next to the grate, listening intently. He heard nothing. It seemed like the perfect moment.

"Now!" Loki yelled. He folded his wings and dropped through the hole, quickly followed by Surt and the other raptors. They fluttered down an old shaft and emerged into a dimly lit tunnel. The ceiling was made of yellow tile that reflected the grimy lights set in the walls. Below them, steel tracks vanished into the distance.

"Where are we?" Surt yelled.

"Beneath the streets!" Loki answered. "The humans have a system of tunnels that can take us anywhere we want to go. Now hurry! We don't have much time."

"What are you afraid of?" Surt asked.

As if in response, the raptors heard a high-pitched squeal behind them. A pair of lights that looked like the eyes of a giant monster appeared in the distance and quickly grew brighter.

"Fly! Fly!" Loki screamed.

The birds furiously beat their wings, following the tunnel as it rounded a bend and widened into an underground station. Startled humans stumbled back as the birds swooped over their heads and landed on a narrow ledge set high in the wall, just as the iron monster roared into the station and came to a stop.

"You fool!" Surt roared. "You almost got us killed!"

"Almost doesn't count," the crow said. "Now come on. We

need to catch a ride." The raptors followed Loki as he flew down and dropped onto the tracks behind the last car of the train. Then they hopped beneath the car and grabbed hold of the undercarriage.

"Now what do we do?" Gunlad asked.

"Now we hang on," Loki replied. "We're about to get the ride of our lives!"

The train suddenly lurched and began to move. Surt and the other raptors tightened their grip and flattened themselves to avoid being blown off by the sheer force of the acceleration. Within seconds, the train was speeding down the tracks. Panic overwhelmed the raptors as their feathers were blasted in every direction. A putrid haze filled the air, tearing at their lungs. It took all of their strength just to breathe.

"Loki, I'm going to kill you for this!" Surt shouted as he stared at the spinning wheels just inches from his head. One wrong move would mean certain death.

After what seemed like hours but was only a few minutes, a light appeared ahead of them and grew brighter. The train suddenly burst out of the tunnel and rocketed over Longfellow Bridge. The birds blinked their eyes in the bright light of day. Beneath them, sailboats glided lazily over the Charles River.

"Look there!" Loki cried.

The raptors followed the crow's gaze. On the bank of the river, they could just make out the sparrows hidden in the trees.

"Don't worry," Loki said. "They're too busy watching the sky to notice us."

The train reached the far side of the bridge, passed the

Winged Regiment, then began to slow. "Follow me!" Loki yelled. The raptors took flight and followed the crow to a patch of trees.

"You fool!" Surt roared as they took refuge amid its branches and greedily gulped the fresh air. "You call that a plan?"

"You wanted to enter the city without being detected," Loki replied smugly. "Mission accomplished. Now stay close and keep low. The Winged Regiment has spies everywhere."

Loki took to the air and headed toward the Boston Common. Surt, Gunlad, and the hawks followed as the crow flew low through side streets and back alleys, always keeping an eye out for signs of the enemy.

As they approached Copley Square, the John Hancock Tower loomed before them, its glass exterior reflecting the city around it.

"We have to reach the top," Loki yelled.

The raptors hurtled forward. Out in the open, they were far better fliers than he was, and the crow soon found himself falling behind. He gasped for breath as he struggled to gain altitude. He finally reached the top of the sixtieth floor and collapsed on the roof.

"What's the matter, crow?" Surt asked. "That little flight wear you out?"

Loki dragged himself to his feet and joined the raptors at the roof's edge. The city of Boston lay before them in a breathtaking panorama. From this vantage point, they could see the sparrows in the trees lining the Charles River, waiting for the birds of prey to cross.

Loki directed their attention to Copley Square. "That belfry is the headquarters of the Feathered Alliance. Hoogol and the rest of the clan leaders will be inside."

"Excellent," Surt said. "You've done well. Now fly to the river and signal the attack."

Blue Feather paced back and forth in the belfry of the Old South Church, careful not to wake the other clan leaders, the majority of whom were still asleep. They had been up late discussing the strengths and weaknesses of various plans in case of an attack. It had been a night of endless bickering. For a long time, nobody could agree on anything. Finally it was decided that the Winged Regiment could hold off the raptors long enough for the leaders to escape, should the need arise.

Blue Feather didn't like the idea of fleeing the city. What if Ragtag returned and they were gone? Nobody had seen or heard from him since last night. Tattler had told her Ragtag had flown off toward the harbor after the clan leaders' departure. He had talked about running away, but Tattler didn't think he would go through with it.

Why did Ragtag have to be so stubborn? Blue Feather couldn't understand his behavior. The idea that he had befriended an eagle was just too hard to believe—yet Tattler had told her she believed him.

Blue Feather fluttered over to the corner of the belfry, where a pair of gulls had stacked branches covered with bayberries. She knew she should eat to keep up her strength, but she had no appetite. She was too worried about Ragtag.

The swallow turned her attention to Hoogol and Proud Beak, who were talking quietly near the wheel. As usual, Bobtail was hovering next to them. If there was anything important going on, Bobtail had to be in the thick of it. Blue Feather knew he dreamt of one day leading the alliance. She was proud of Bobtail's ambitions, but she wished he would express a bit more concern for his own brother.

Blue Feather crossed to a window and looked down at the library. For a brief moment, she half expected to see Ragtag sunning himself atop the roof, as he did most mornings. Her spirits sank when she didn't.

"There's nothing you can do, Mom," Bobtail said behind her. "It's no good worrying."

"I'm a nervous wreck," Blue Feather said as her son approached. "I'm afraid Ragtag's run off for good."

"Bah!" Bobtail replied, sounding just like Proud Beak. "He's just sulking. No doubt he'll fly back when he gets hungry."

Blue Feather glanced at Proud Beak and Hoogol, then lowered her voice. "You're very close to Proud Beak. Isn't there anything you can do? Perhaps a well-placed word . . ."

Bobtail rolled his eyes. "In case you haven't noticed, Mom, we're a bit busy. I don't think now would be a good time to mention Ragtag's name."

"But what if the raptors invade? What if we're forced to flee?"

"Don't worry. I'm sure Ragtag and his imaginary eagle can take care of themselves."

"Bobtail, get over here!" Proud Beak called from across the room.

"I have to go," Bobtail said quickly to his mother. "Don't tell anybody this, but I think Hoogol may make me third-in-command of the Feathered Alliance!"

Bobtail turned and hurried back to Proud Beak and Hoogol. Blue Feather sighed and shook her head. Perhaps Bobtail was right. Maybe Ragtag had to learn to take care of himself. Determined not to worry any more about Ragtag, Blue Feather turned and hopped away from the window.

She just missed seeing Loki heading for the river.

Ragtag glided aimlessly over the streets lining the city's waterfront. Now that he had been banished from the alliance, he had all the time in the world. There was nobody to tell him what to do and—best of all—nobody to yell at him or call him irresponsible. He should have been the happiest bird in the world. So why wasn't he?

The swallow scanned the streets beneath him. He had never seen the clans in such a state. Some, like the finches and the robins, were busy hoarding food and camouflaging their nests. Others, like the blackbirds and the magpies, had given up all hope and were abandoning their homes. Parents tried desperately to keep their young ones together as hundreds of families took to the sky and headed south in droves.

Ragtag's thoughts turned to his own family. They were probably busy helping Hoogol and Proud Beak. No doubt Bobtail was having the time of his life, pretending to be infinitely more important than he really was.

He fluttered down to a park bench and watched as a

flock of sparrows headed west to reinforce those already encamped by the river. Ragtag was seized with the sudden urge to join them, but he knew that if he did, he would just be in the way. Swallows weren't allowed in the Winged Regiment. They were too slow to be of any real use in a fight.

As he watched the birds around him, Ragtag began to realize the full magnitude of what was about to happen. For the first time in his life, he felt truly afraid.

He closed his eyes and dreamt he was lost in a vast labyrinth. From somewhere ahead of him came the cry of an eagle. Ragtag flew through the maze, desperately calling Baldur's name. But every time he thought he'd spotted him, it turned out to be nothing more than a shadow.

"What are they waiting for?" Headstrong asked. "I wish they would just get it over with. Why don't they attack?"

"They will when they're ready," Tattler replied as she watched him spread his wings. "Where are you going?"

"To inspect the troops."

"You've done that five times in the last hour."

"It gives me something to do," Headstrong muttered. "It's better than just sitting around here waiting for our funeral."

As Tattler watched him fly off, her thoughts drifted back to the time she had narrowly defeated him in the competition to determine the leadership of the Winged Regiment. Instead of holding a grudge, he had become her most loyal friend and adviser. Headstrong trusted her, and she hoped with all her heart she wouldn't let him down.

Tattler's claws tightened on the branch beneath her. Why

didn't they attack? Headstrong was right. Being forced to sit around and do nothing was unbearable. She thought she would lose her mind if she had to wait much longer.

As it turned out, she didn't have to wait long at all. A cry of alarm was suddenly raised by the sparrows in the surrounding trees. Loki zoomed past her and headed out over the water. Halfway across the river, he banked left and flew parallel to the shore.

"Caw-caw!" the crow screamed at the top of his lungs.

His cry was picked up by the raptors hidden on the opposite shore, the screeches sending a chill through the sparrows. They watched as the birds of prey took to the air and began to cross the river.

Tattler took a deep breath. "This is it!" she called. Instantly, hundreds of sparrows launched themselves from the surrounding trees.

Tattler and Headstrong skimmed low over the waves, furiously flapping their wings to gain as much speed as possible. Behind them, the Winged Regiment spread out to make their numbers appear greater.

A great cry arose from the Talon Empire as they spotted their opponents. Hawks, harriers, ospreys, and falcons screamed in anticipation of the battle.

In the middle of the river, a fisherman in a rowboat cast his rod. He glanced up at the sky and toppled back in shock. Above him, the Winged Regiment collided with the birds of prey. The sudden mass of wings and feathers blotted out the sun.

High above the river, Tattler darted about, beak snapping. Talons slashed at her, but the sparrow was too quick. She bolted away as a hawk shrieked in rage. Beating her wings, she flew higher and fell in next to a pair of her comrades.

"Follow me!" Tattler yelled over the screams below. The sparrows nodded, frantically trying to keep up with their leader.

The three birds climbed into the sky, then suddenly reversed course and dove toward an osprey. They closed ranks and collided as one, breaking the osprey's back. The impact knocked Tattler senseless for a moment. She shook her head, then watched as the osprey hit the water and sank out of sight.

"First blood to us!" Tattler yelled.

A falcon screamed and shot toward her. Tattler banked to one side, wincing in pain as she lost a few feathers. She darted through the mass of fighting birds, then doubled back and rammed the falcon. The raptor shrugged her off as if she were a mosquito.

A heartrending cry from below suddenly stopped Tattler in midair. She watched in horror as a northern goshawk pursued a wounded sparrow. A dozen members of the Winged Regiment tried to come to the sparrow's aid, but the goshawk plowed through them.

"Climb, you fool!" Tattler called, and dove toward the terrified bird, even though she knew there was no way she could reach him in time.

"Save me! Save me!" the sparrow called to his comrades as he rose toward the sun in a vain attempt to blind his opponent.

"There'll be no saving you!" the goshawk snarled. His

talons slashed the sparrow's back, and the wounded bird dropped like a rock.

"No!" Tattler cried. She closed her eyes as the sparrow slammed into the river, sending a plume of water three feet into the air.

"We're getting massacred out here!" Headstrong yelled as he flew up beside Tattler.

"We have no choice!" Tattler said. "Keep at them. We need to give the clan leaders time to escape."

Headstrong nodded and dove back into the fray. As Tattler evaded a harrier's snapping beak, she realized with a sinking heart that it was hopeless. The battle was already lost.

Proud Beak

The Fall of the Belfry

Ragtag heard the cry of a terrified seagull and shook himself awake. He jumped out from under the bench as gulls circled and wheeled overhead. Others were anxiously hopping back and forth along the piers. He knew gulls acted like that only when there was danger.

The swallow flew up to a roof for a better view. A pair of starlings turned to him with terror in their eyes.

"What is it?" Ragtag asked.

"The birds of prey are crossing the river," one of the starlings replied, her voice shaking.

"The Winged Regiment will stop them," chirped her companion.

"You're a fool!" a gull declared, fluttering down between them. "Everyone knows that sparrows are no match for raptors."

"What about our nests?" the female starling cried. "Who'll protect our young?"

Ragtag was left to ponder the question alone as the birds

took to the air. He watched them head south, then looked back at the river. Far in the distance, he could make out hundreds of birds over the water. His stomach turned to lead as he watched the Winged Regiment engaging the birds of prey. Even though Ragtag knew he wasn't fast or nimble enough for combat, he wasn't about to sit back and do nothing. He headed for the river as fast as his wings could carry him.

Inside the belfry of the Old South Church, the clan leaders were in a state of panic. They rushed about in all directions, tripping over each other in their haste to escape. Nobody had expected the attack to come so soon.

"The birds of prey are crossing the river!" Gini screamed.

"The city is being invaded!" Proud Beak yelled.

"We're doomed!" Bragi moaned.

Hoogol flapped his wings for silence. "Stay calm! The Winged Regiment will slow down any invasion long enough for us to evacuate."

Blue Feather rushed over to Bobtail. "What about Ragtag?"

"He'll have to take care of himself. Come on, Mom, we need to leave."

Bobtail and Blue Feather hurried over to Hoogol and Proud Beak, who had finally gotten the pigeons under control. But just as they were about to depart, Gini screamed, and they all whirled to see Surt landing on the southern entrance of the belfry.

Hoogol's blood ran cold. "The enemy is upon us!" he thundered. "Fly! Fly!"

Surt hopped inside, causing the panicking leaders to

bump into one another. Bobtail pushed Blue Feather behind him as the peregrine's beak snapped at the terrified birds.

"Everyone, follow me!" Proud Beak cried, taking flight and heading for the north window. Gunlad suddenly blocked the exit, his talons raking the cardinal. Proud Beak squawked in pain and stumbled back.

The desperate birds glanced at the two remaining windows just as red-tailed hawks landed on both entrances and hopped inside. Bragi and the pigeons hid their heads under their wings as Surt moved forward.

"Which of you is Hoogol?" the falcon asked loudly.

"I'm Hoogol," Proud Beak declared, hopping in front of the great horned owl.

"Proud Beak, my friend, it's no use," Hoogol said. Proud Beak tried to protest, but Hoogol gently pushed him aside. The owl drew himself up to his full height and faced Surt. "I'm Hoogol."

"So this is the leader of the great Feathered Alliance," Surt cackled. "An old, worn-out owl." The falcon walked forward until they were standing eye to eye. Hoogol didn't flinch under the peregrine's steely gaze.

"What do you want of us?" Hoogol asked.

"You will send one of your pigeons to the river and order the sparrows to surrender," Surt replied.

"No, no!" the pigeons chanted, but were quickly silenced by the hawks.

"And if we refuse?" Hoogol asked.

"If you refuse," Surt continued, "my raptors will kill your

birds one by one." He glanced at the pigeons. "Starting with the tasty-looking ones."

Surt kept his penetrating gaze on Hoogol as the terrified pigeons peeked out from under their wings. Finally the old owl bowed his head. "Bragi, fly to the river and order the Winged Regiment to stand down."

"What?" Proud Beak protested. "Hoogol, no!"

"The sparrows will be destroyed," Bobtail said.

"No! No!" Bragi cried. "I won't do it."

"You must," Hoogol said. "The sparrows will be killed if you don't. And us along with them. Now do as I say, before it's too late."

Surt turned to Gunlad. "Escort this quivering sack of feathers to the river. If she strays in any way, kill her."

Bragi took to the air and left the belfry behind, the hawk on her tail. The pigeon was so frightened she could barely fly straight. It was only a short flight from the Old South Church to the Charles River, yet it felt like the longest distance she had ever flown in her life.

The sun reflected off the water ahead of them. Birds of all shapes and sizes were still aloft. The ranks of the Winged Regiment had been decimated, yet the sparrows refused to give up.

Bragi landed on the branch of a nearby tree and shouted to the sparrows still engaged in battle over the river. "Stand down! Stand down! Hoogol orders the Winged Regiment to surrender!"

A sparrow took up the cry, followed by another and another. Gradually, the injured and exhausted birds fell back to the trees lining the bank.

Tattler landed on a branch next to Bragi. "What's happened?"

"The belfry has fallen!" Bragi sobbed.

"But that's impossible! How could they have gotten behind us?"

"We've been betrayed," Headstrong said as he landed next to them.

"Hoogol orders the Winged Regiment to surrender," Bragi continued, her voice shaking.

A cry of despair went through the sparrows as the news quickly spread. The birds of prey landed in the trees next to them, forcing them closer together. Gunlad spread his wings to gain their attention.

"The battle is over!" he yelled. "The leaders of the Feathered Alliance have been captured. Any sparrow who takes to the air will be brought down immediately."

Tattler and Headstrong exchanged a horrified look. Could the birds of prey have outwitted them so easily? Dozens of raptors were landing on the outer branches of the trees. The subdued and hesitant sparrows were slowly being forced toward the center. It would be only seconds until they were all trapped.

"I don't care if they've captured the belfry!" Tattler shouted. "We may have lost this battle, but the Winged Regiment will never surrender. All sparrows, scatter!"

Instantly a hundred sparrows bolted away in all directions. The birds of prey spread their wings to give chase.

Tattler launched herself from her perch, dove low, and skimmed across the grass.

Gunlad turned to a harrier. "Kill her."

"With pleasure," the harrier said, and took to the air.

Tattler darted in and out of the trees lining the river. She glanced behind her, her spirits sinking as she realized the bird of prey was quickly closing the gap.

"Heads up!" the harrier taunted.

The sparrow looked ahead and quickly swerved to avoid plowing into a billboard.

Calm down, Tattler told herself. Panicking will only get you killed. He's stronger and faster, but not smarter!

She changed direction and shot skyward. Higher and higher Tattler climbed, the rooftops of the city dropping away.

"You're a fool to leave the ground," the harrier yelled. "You can't outfly me!"

In the open sky, with nothing to impede his flight, the harrier's longer wingspan allowed him to close the gap easily. The raptor shot forward, talons snapping so close to Tattler they pulled out one of her tail feathers.

Suddenly Tattler folded her wings and dove toward the roof of a building far below; the harrier followed. Both birds pressed their wings to their bodies as they plummeted faster and faster.

Please let this work, Tattler thought as the wind whistled through her feathers. Her eyes shrank to a pair of slits as the roof rushed toward her. At the very last second, she banked.

Behind her, the raptor tried to match the maneuver, but his

size and weight were too much. The harrier slammed into the rooftop at over sixty miles an hour as Tattler veered safely away.

Ragtag flew as fast as he could through the canyons created by the city's skyscrapers. News of the battle over the river and the invasion of the raptors had spread like wildfire. Terrified birds were scattering in all directions.

The swallow squinted to shield his eyes from the glare of the sun. He could no longer see any birds over the river. Worried sick over what might have happened to Blue Feather, Bobtail, and Tattler, he decided to head back to the belfry. He knew it would be a risk. He had been banished and warned to stay away, but he no longer cared. He had to find out what was happening. He increased his speed, pushing his wings to their limit. He was so intent on reaching home that he didn't notice another bird closing in fast.

Suddenly he was rammed from behind. His assailant locked her claws onto him, and the two birds spiraled down out of the sky. Wings fluttered wildly to break their fall, and they both landed in a patch of soft grass. Ragtag sprang to his feet and turned to face his attacker.

"Tattler!" Ragtag cried out in surprise.

Tattler jumped atop him and dragged him out of sight.

"Hush," she warned. "Not a word."

Ragtag followed the sparrow's gaze up to the sky. They could just make out the distinct silhouette of a raptor floating quietly overhead.

"What is it?" Ragtag whispered.

"Kestrel," Tattler grunted.

Ragtag's blood ran cold. A kestrel was a sparrow hawk. They were notorious hunters, often hovering in one place for hours before diving out of the sky to capture their prey.

"We can't stay here," Tattler said quietly. "Follow me and stay close to the ground. And, Ragtag, whatever happens, don't look back."

Ragtag was full of questions, but a stern glance from Tattler told him that now was not the time. The sparrow took to the air and skimmed over the grass. With a pounding heart, Ragtag followed. What was a kestrel doing so close to the Old South Church? Where was the Winged Regiment?

It was all Ragtag could do to keep up with Tattler as she led them through the underbrush. She landed near a fence and waited for him.

Ragtag finally caught up with her. Across from them was the Boston Common and the Public Garden. Lush fields of grass lay between groves of woods that surrounded a shimmering lake. Breathing heavily, he watched in disbelief as Tattler once again spread her wings.

"Are you crazy?" Ragtag whispered. "We'll be spotted if we try to cross the common!"

"We have no choice," Tattler replied.

Ragtag took a deep breath and followed her over the exposed fields. The shrill cry of the kestrel came from above. The raptor's keen eyesight had picked up on their movement. It folded its wings and dove toward them.

"Hurry!" Tattler yelled as she headed for a corner of the park. A dozen pigeons were gathered around an old human who was sitting on a bench feeding them.

The two birds landed and quickly blended in with the crowd. The pigeons were trembling and muttering to themselves.

"We're doomed," one of the birds moaned.

"Shut up!" Tattler ordered. She hopped over to Ragtag, who was looking warily at the old lady. He was uncomfortable being this close to a human. The woman smiled at the newcomers and threw down some seed.

"Food?" Ragtag muttered. "Who could eat at a time like this?"

"Ragtag, look," Tattler said.

The birds watched in horror as the kestrel landed on a lamp overlooking the bench. The raptor folded its wings and glared at them, its eyes going from the birds to the human, then back to the birds.

The pigeons huddled closer together. Growing bolder, the kestrel fluttered down and alighted next to the old lady. She gave a start as she caught sight of the bird of prey. With one look, she could easily guess its intent.

"You foul-smelling, dirty-minded little monster!" she yelled. "Get away from my birds!"

The kestrel flapped its wings in an attempt to drive away the human, but the old lady wasn't so easily intimidated. She grabbed her bags and swung them. The raptor screamed in rage before taking flight and vanishing into the sky.

"We're saved!" a pigeon cried.

"Saved! Saved!" the others warbled, crowding even closer around the old woman's feet.

"I thought it would never leave," Ragtag said.

Tattler addressed the pigeons. "Everyone, listen to me! The Talon Empire has taken control of the city, and the Winged Regiment has gone into hiding. I advise you all to do the same."

"Leave our protector?" a fat pigeon cried out from the back of the flock.

"Never!" responded another.

"She'll care for us," said a third.

"She won't let us be eaten," added a fourth.

Tattler exchanged a knowing glance with Ragtag. Pigeons were faint-hearted even at the best of times. Not in a million years would they be persuaded to leave the safety of the old lady, especially with a kestrel on the loose.

"Suit yourself," Tattler said, and motioned for Ragtag to follow her. They flew a short distance to the shelter offered by a hedge.

"Tattler, what happened?" Ragtag asked. He had a million questions, and they began spilling out. "How could the raptors take the city so fast?"

"They somehow got behind our lines without us knowing it," Tattler replied.

"But how?"

"I don't know, but they did it." Tattler anxiously hopped back and forth. "Ragtag, they launched a surprise attack on the belfry! Hoogol and the clan leaders have been taken prisoner."

Ragtag stumbled back as if hit by lightning. If the birds of prey had taken the belfry, that meant his mother and brother were captives.

"Bobtail! Mom!" he cried. He spread his wings. Tattler quickly hopped atop him and pushed him down.

"Let me go!" Ragtag said. "They need my help."

"There's nothing you can do."

"They'll be killed!"

"So will you if you foolishly fly up there. It would be suicide to go against those raptors."

"But—but— We can't just give up!"

"And we won't, but we have to use our brains. Trust me, Ragtag. Secret messages have already been sent, but we can't risk flying during the day. We have to wait until dark."

Romeo & Juliet

The Bridge in the Garden

B irds of prey quickly seized control of the city's skyscrapers. Hawks perched high overhead, their keen eyes gazing at the streets below for any sign of the sparrows. Harriers and merlins patrolled the city's airspace in groups of four, flying in formation as they kept an eye on those clans who hadn't been lucky enough to have escaped.

Bergelmir was escorted across the river by Gunlad and his hawks. Loki trailed them at a respectable distance as they headed for Copley Square. The raptors circled the belfry of the Old South Church before landing on its ledge. Surt bowed low as Bergelmir hopped inside.

"Well done, Surt!" the emperor said as he headed for the corner where the clan leaders were being held.

Fear spread through the prisoners at the sight of the osprey. Only Hoogol and Proud Beak glared defiantly at the emperor. Bergelmir paid the cardinal no attention. He moved in front of Hoogol as the great horned owl drew himself up to his full height.

"We meet again, Hoogol," said the osprey.

The other birds exchanged a startled glance. Hoogol had never mentioned knowing Bergelmir.

"Age hasn't been good to you," Bergelmir continued. "You look old and weak, my friend."

"I am not your friend!" Hoogol thundered. His eyes flashed and his wings trembled. Surt and Gunlad jumped forward, ready to defend their emperor. For a second, the clan leaders thought Hoogol would strike, but the old owl quickly mastered his emotions and turned away.

"Once again, you show your cowardice," Bergelmir said with a sneer. "You were a coward the last time we met, and you are a coward now."

"They didn't even put up a fight," Surt said, indicating the clan leaders.

"Of course not," Bergelmir replied. "That's because they're weak. Isn't that right, Hoogol?"

Hoogol held his head high as he stared down the osprey. "If you consider my devotion to the safety and well-being of these birds weakness, then yes. I am weak."

"You're not only weak, you're pathetic!" Bergelmir laughed. "We should have destroyed this miserable alliance of yours a long time ago."

The clan leaders gasped as Loki suddenly landed in the belfry.

"Traitor!" Proud Beak roared, and launched himself at the crow. He never made it. With a flash of feathers, Surt came to Loki's defense. The falcon's talons instantly brought the cardinal down.

"Proud Beak, no!" Blue Feather cried.

It was too late. Proud Beak was dead before he hit the floor. Loki hopped back and swallowed nervously. The hostages trembled as Surt hovered over the cardinal's body. Even Gunlad's hawks seemed stunned to see the full might of the peregrine falcon unleashed.

"Let that be a lesson to all of you!" Bergelmir said as he walked from bird to bird. "Are there any more heroes among you? Come forth if you wish to test yourself against the heir to my throne!"

The birds cowered in fear and averted their gaze. Bergelmir finally came full circle and stopped once again in front of Hoogol.

"What about you? Do you care to test yourself against Surt? Or perhaps the city has tamed even a great horned owl?"

Hoogol's eyes blazed with fury, but in the end, he, too, looked away.

"I thought as much," Bergelmir said with satisfaction. He addressed Loki. "You've kept your part of the bargain, and I shall keep mine. Leave us now. The crows shall remain free."

Loki nodded. He took one last look at Proud Beak's body and headed for the window.

"Enjoy your freedom, Loki," Hoogol said quietly as the crow was about to depart. "We paid a terrible price for it."

Loki hesitated, then spread his wings and took flight.

I did what I had to do, Loki thought as he left the belfry behind. The image of Proud Beak's body was stuck in his mind. The crow shook himself, angry that he was feeling pity for

Hoogol and the others. He reminded himself that the Feathered Alliance was an enemy of the crows.

Loki kept a low profile as he flew west from Copley Square. Raptors were everywhere, attacking birds and overturning nests, all in their search for the scattered sparrows. The crow banked and dropped toward a set of train tracks. A hawk spotted him and charged forward to intercept, only to turn away as it recognized him. The raptors were keeping Bergelmir's promise.

Loki let out a sigh of relief and followed the tracks north. Ahead of him lay South Station, a train terminal the crows used for a meeting place. A distant "caw-caw" greeted him as a pair of his cousins rose and joined him on either side.

The crows escorted Loki to an old locomotive that had been abandoned in a distant corner of the yard. More than two dozen crows sat atop it, waiting for their leader's arrival. Loki landed and was instantly mobbed by the crowd.

"You did it!" one of his flock congratulated him.

"We have free rein over the city!" another cackled.

An old crow named Garm hopped forward. "Congratulations, Loki. Your plan worked. The raptors are enslaving what remains of the Feathered Alliance, but we are free!"

"Don't be fooled," Loki snapped, surprised by the anger in his own voice. "The empire is still a threat to us. Fafnir! Gungmir!"

Loki's two younger brothers hopped forward.

"You're the best spies we have," Loki said. "I want you to keep an eye on Bergelmir. I need to know every move the emperor makes. Can I count on you?"

"Of course, brother!" Fafnir said.

"He won't see us, but we'll see him," Gungmir added.

Loki watched as they headed west toward Copley Square.

Night fell over the city. The Boston Common was seemingly deserted. Wind whistled through the trees and sent ripples across the grass.

A northern goshawk soared over the open area, scanning the fields and trees with her keen eyes. There was no sign of life. The goshawk beat her wings and vanished into the distance.

"Is she gone?" Ragtag asked as Tattler hopped out from their hiding place.

"Yes, I think so. Come on!"

Together the two birds flew over the Public Garden and landed at the edge of a small pond. Tattler quietly chirped across the water as Ragtag watched curiously.

"Where are they?" the sparrow muttered.

"Where are who?" asked Ragtag.

Tattler ignored him and chirped again, her claw tapping impatiently on the ground. Still there was no response. Ragtag was growing restless when the sparrow suddenly said, "About time they showed up!"

A pair of swans appeared on the water and glided in their direction.

"Romeo and Juliet are rather shy around strangers," Tattler whispered to Ragtag. "I think it's better if you let me do the talking."

The swallow nodded and watched with fascination as the

swans moved toward them. He had seen Romeo and Juliet before, but never up close, and he had never dared talk to them.

The swans weren't members of the Feathered Alliance. Although they were treated with respect by the birds of the city, they preferred to keep to themselves. Everyone knew that there was some sort of strange agreement between them and the humans. Every winter the humans would come and take them away, only to return them to the Boston Public Garden in the spring. Most of the clans tended to treat the swans with a bit of suspicion. They didn't act like proper birds. Even their names were foreign and given to them by the humans.

Romeo and Juliet glided silently to the edge of the water. They lowered their slender heads as Ragtag and Tattler hopped closer.

"Thanks for coming," Tattler said.

"You're welcome, Tattler, dear," Juliet replied. Her voice was soft and lush, exactly what Ragtag would have expected a swan to sound like.

"Have the others arrived?" Tattler asked.

"Yes," Romeo said. "Everyone's gathered under the bridge, ol' girl. But be careful—there are hawks in the trees to the north."

"Thank you. The alliance is in your debt."

"The pleasure is ours," Juliet replied.

"Indeed it is," Romeo added. "Those raptors are an uncivilized lot."

"Disagreeable creatures," Juliet said as she nestled closer to her mate. "Heaven help us if we had to live with them . . ."

"Simply couldn't stand for it," Romeo agreed.

"Come on, Ragtag," Tattler said, and took to the air as the swans glided away. Ragtag followed the sparrow as she skimmed across the water. An ornate stone bridge spanned the narrowest part of the lake. A motley band of city birds had taken shelter on the ground beneath it. The bridge shielded them from the view of any raptors flying overhead.

Ragtag and Tattler landed and joined the crowd. They were greeted with cries of astonishment. Headstrong pushed his way forward, a look of joy on his face. "Tattler! We thought you were dead. They told us a harrier caught you!"

"The only thing that harrier caught was a roof," Tattler replied. "Quickly now, we don't have much time. How bad is it?"

Headstrong's happiness vanished. "It's bad. Only half the clans managed to escape. The others are under the control of the raptors. Bergelmir has posted sentries atop all the skyscrapers. The hawks can see for miles. Any bird caught flying without permission is immediately attacked and brought down."

"What about my mother?" Ragtag asked. "What about Bobtail?"

"They're alive," Headstrong replied, "but they've been taken hostage, along with Hoogol and the rest. The raptors have moved them to the attic of the church. I guess they figured the belfry was too hard to defend."

"Something we should have known!" Tattler said. "What about the Winged Regiment?"

"The birds of prey chased us after you gave the order to

scatter. We lost quite a few, but the majority managed to escape and are hiding outside the city."

"Since Bergelmir controls the sky now, I take it there's no easy way to communicate with them?"

Headstrong nodded. Behind him, a group of robins had been listening with growing anxiety. One of them finally spoke up. "Our nests are unprotected, and we have young waiting to be fed. Can't we negotiate with this Bergelmir?"

"We have nothing to negotiate with," Tattler replied.

Ragtag hopped forward as the birds twittered nervously. He had been listening quietly in the background, but now an idea was beginning to take shape in his mind. "If the Winged Regiment were somehow able to regroup, could they launch a new attack against the empire?"

Tattler and Headstrong exchanged a startled glance.

"Perhaps," Tattler said, "but what would be the point?"

"Tattler's right," Headstrong agreed. "As long as Bergelmir holds Hoogol and the clan leaders hostage, we can't risk it."

"Then it's obvious what we have to do," Ragtag said. "We have to rescue them!"

For a split second, there was a stunned silence. Then everyone started talking.

"You're insane!" Kittiwook declared, pushing her way forward. The mockingbird was one of the luckier clan leaders. She had been out with her children looking for berries when Surt and the other raptors took the belfry. "They're too powerful! It would be mad to attempt a rescue."

"Mad! Mad!" the pigeons chortled.

"Hush!" Tattler said. "Ragtag, there are more than a dozen

raptors guarding the hostages. How do you propose we rescue them? Do you think we're just going to walk into Bergelmir's lair and sneak them out one by one?"

Ragtag gave Tattler a knowing look, and the sparrow guessed exactly what he was thinking.

"That's exactly what we're going to do!" he announced.

"I still don't understand," Headstrong said, shaking his head. "Even if we could get inside the church, how would we find our way up to the attic?"

"That's the easy part," Ragtag replied.

"Easy?" Headstrong stared at him in astonishment.

"It should be. After all, I was born there."

Blackcap

The Old South Church

As morning's first light spread over the city, Copley Square began to bustle with life. Humans were hurrying every which way across the plaza. As they crossed in front of the Old South Church, they had no idea they were being watched.

A pair of hawks stood guard on the roof. Beneath them, a young kestrel named Hod peered out from a window in the attic. He watched with disdain as the humans went about their business. Somewhere in the distance, a car horn honked. The kestrel took a nervous step back.

Hod hated the city. He couldn't understand why humans chose to live in such a place. The endless barrage of sights and sounds gave him a headache. He longed to return to the quiet of the forest.

Turning his back on the square, Hod saw Hoogol and the clan leaders huddled in a corner of the dusty attic. Bergelmir, Surt, and the rest of the raptors sat in the center of the chamber, feasting on mice, rats, and fish that had been brought to them earlier in the morning.

A flutter of movement caused Hod to whirl around. The emperor's bodyguards, twin sister merlins named Hugin and Munin, flew in through the window and landed next to Bergelmir. They were small and compact, about the length of a jay, with dusty brown feathers and banded tails. The two sisters bowed low.

"Well, don't just stand there," Bergelmir said. "Report!"

"Unfortunate news from Gunlad, m'lord," said Hugin.

"The sparrows have escaped," said Munin.

"Order Gunlad to track them down!" Surt snapped.

"That would be difficult, if not impossible," replied Hugin.

"They've fled the city and scattered in all directions," added Munin.

"I don't care where they're hiding!" Bergelmir roared. "Tell Gunlad not to show his face until he's found them and killed them!"

"As you wish," Hugin said, and took wing along with her sister.

As the raptors returned to their meal, Bobtail tried to comfort his mother on the other side of the attic.

"I—I keep thinking about Proud Beak," Blue Feather sobbed.

"At least the sparrows escaped," Bobtail muttered as he watched Surt rip apart a dead rat. As the peregrine thrust back his head and swallowed a chunk of meat whole, Bobtail was overcome with rage and disgust. The clan leaders were starving. The raptors had promised to bring them berries, but that promise had yet to be fulfilled.

Bobtail wished he was strong enough to challenge the falcon, but there was nothing he could do. There was nothing any of them could do. He doubted even Hoogol would last long against Surt.

"What about Ragtag?" Blue Feather whispered, her voice cracking. "What if he comes back?"

"I'm sure he's smart enough to keep his distance." Bobtail fell silent as a pair of kestrels stalked past. The prisoners had quickly learned to fear the sparrow hawks. Even though they were no larger than pigeons, they had talons as sharp as knives, and no qualms about using them.

Gini hurried over as soon as the kestrels had moved away. "Why doesn't Hoogol do something?" the starling whispered.

"Like what?" Bobtail asked.

"I don't know, but we can't just sit here. We've got to try to make a run for it. One of us should cause a distraction."

"You volunteering?"

Gini scowled and hopped away. Bragi stirred and restlessly flapped her wings. "We're doomed."

"Doomed! Doomed!" the pigeons cooed.

"Quiet!" Bobtail whispered, but it was too late.

Surt glanced up from his meal. "Shut up, you!"

The pigeons cried even more loudly. Surt got to his feet and moved forward. "I said shut up!"

Hoogol suddenly blocked Surt's advance. The falcon's eyes narrowed, his talons opened, and his wings spread wide. He was just about to launch himself at the owl when Bergelmir interceded. "Surt, back off."

"What are you going to do with us?" Hoogol asked as the osprey walked over.

"You'll be kept here for as long as it takes to round up the Winged Regiment."

The hostages exchanged excited whispers.

"I wouldn't get your hopes up," Bergelmir said more loudly. "Your sparrows have fled the city like the cowards they are. I doubt they or your clans will try anything as long as you're here."

"It's a pity the emperor wishes you kept alive," Surt added. "These city mice are rather tasteless." The falcon stared hungrily at Bragi as she cowered against the wall.

"You have no right to treat us like this!" Hoogol thundered. "We did you no harm. You have no right to invade our home!"

"Rights?" Bergelmir laughed. "You talk to me of rights? You and your kind have lived here far too long, Hoogol. You've forgotten the way of nature. We are raptors. We rule because we were born to rule. We displace you from your homes the same way the humans displaced us from ours!"

Bergelmir was watching Hoogol with a critical eye. "You yourself, Hoogol, are a bird of prey. I wonder . . . why would a great horned owl associate with these sniveling cowards?"

"You're wrong in thinking they are cowards," Hoogol said. "But you are right about one thing. I have lived away from nature for a long time. Long enough to learn compassion."

Gunlad and the hawks howled in amusement.

"Listen to the way he speaks!" Bergelmir said. "He's as

pretentious as he is stubborn." The osprey glared at Hoogol. "For all your noble aspirations, old owl, you are still a flesh eater. You feel the excitement of the hunt as we do, you ruthlessly track down your prey as we do, and you take your greatest pleasure in the kill as we do!"

"I hunt for food, not pleasure," Hoogol replied. "And that, old osprey, is the difference between me and you."

"Spoken like a weakling."

Bobtail angrily pushed his way forward. He didn't care if the osprey cut him down. He couldn't stand there idly as they insulted his idol.

"Hoogol is not a weakling!" he squeaked. "He's the bravest leader the city has ever known. And he's more than a match for the likes of you!"

The osprey glared at him, and Bobtail quickly hopped back.

"Brave?" Bergelmir sneered. "I wonder, Hoogol, do these birds know exactly how you came to their city? Have you told them the truth about you and me, and how brave you truly are?"

A hundred questions raced through Bobtail's mind as Hoogol remained silent. What was Bergelmir talking about?

"Well, Hoogol?" Bergelmir mocked. "Do you still wish to play the role of the fearless leader?"

The birds watched in horror as Hoogol bowed his head.

"I thought as much," Bergelmir said with satisfaction.

Ragtag, Kittiwook, and four chickadees emerged from beneath the shelter of a tree next to the Old South Church.

They gazed fearfully at the hawks standing guard high above them.

"They're watching the humans," Ragtag said.

"How can you be so sure?" Kittiwook asked.

"Only one way to find out."

Ragtag slowly made his way down the sidewalk. The other birds held their breath as they glanced at the roof. Ragtag was out in the open and vulnerable.

Just stay calm, he told himself. Every instinct told him to take to the air, but he knew the motion would attract the hawks. They were looking for fliers, not walkers. As long as he remained on the ground and moved slowly, they wouldn't see him. At least, that was what he told himself. He expected to hear the terrifying screech of a raptor at any second.

But it never came. Kittiwook and the chickadees sighed in relief as Ragtag reached a bush on the far side of the church and quickly ducked beneath it.

"I'm next," the mockingbird said, and began the trek down the sidewalk.

The chickadees exchanged nervous glances as they watched her cross. They were brothers, and all had volunteered for this mission. Ragtag had initially not wanted them, but Tattler had convinced him to bring them along. Although they were too small to be of any real use against the raptors, they still wanted to contribute in whatever way they could.

"Come on," said Blackcap, who was the oldest. Together the four birds hopped out and headed for the shelter of the shrubbery.

The hawks above them showed no sign of seeing them, and one by one, the chickadees joined Ragtag and Kittiwook under the bush.

"You know what you have to do?" Ragtag asked the mockingbird.

"I won't let you down," Kittiwook replied.

"Good luck."

"And to you! Don't worry, Ragtag, we'll get them out."

Ragtag nodded. He was trying to look as confident as the mockingbird sounded, but deep inside, he wondered if he had what it would take to pull off the rescue. He wished Tattler and Headstrong were with him, but they had a different role to play.

"All right, follow me and keep your voices down," Ragtag said to the chickadees. He stared at the roof, waiting for the right moment to make his move. Seconds later, the hawks were distracted by the honk of a car horn.

Quickly Ragtag spread his wings and flew up to a door in the side of the church. The chickadees followed single file. Above the door, a window was open a crack—just enough for the small birds to squeeze through. They left Kittiwook behind and entered the Old South Church.

A dark hall stretched in front of them. The swallow beat his wings, hovering as he checked for signs of life. From somewhere in the distance came the monotonous drone of a human voice.

Blackcap's heart was beating so fast he thought it would explode. It was the first time he or any of his brothers had been indoors. As they followed Ragtag down the deserted corridor and up a wooden staircase, he had to fight the urge to panic and flee.

The staircase opened onto a pulpit overlooking the vast interior of the church. The awestruck chickadees landed next to Ragtag as the human droned away at the front of the chamber. Dozens of other humans sat listening, most either asleep or staring vacantly into space.

Memories came flooding back to Ragtag. On the opposite side of the church was the large marble statue behind which he and Bobtail had been born. At the time, the other swallows had told Blue Feather that it was too dangerous to build a nest inside a human dwelling, but she couldn't be dissuaded. The warmth and the shelter from the elements were too attractive.

Blackcap prodded Ragtag. The swallow shook himself and turned his attention to the vaulted ceiling. This was no time for daydreams. Blue Feather and Bobtail were being held captive by the birds of prey somewhere above them.

"Follow me," Ragtag whispered, and took to the air. He flew up and landed along a narrow ledge that ran the length of the ceiling, the chickadees so close behind him that they kept bumping into his tail.

Please let it be here, he thought as he hopped forward. As a fledgling, he had explored every nook and cranny of this church with Tattler. Long ago, they had discovered a small opening in the ceiling's masonry that led to the upper rafters. Now he knew it was the only way this rescue team could get into the attic without alerting the raptors.

Relief washed over Ragtag as he spotted the opening

above him. He slipped through and waited for Blackcap and his brothers. Then they all waited until their eyes adjusted to the dim light.

Dust drifted through the rafters overhead. The chickadees followed Ragtag as he hopped from beam to beam, slowly working his way up until he reached a crawlspace directly beneath the attic.

Blackcap suddenly chirped from too much excitement. *"Chikadee-dee-dee!"*

"Hush!" Ragtag warned. "Do you want to give us away?"

"Sorry, Ragtag, I couldn't help it," Blackcap whispered, his face crestfallen.

The birds waited anxiously, but no sound came from above. Ragtag moved forward and finally found what he was looking for: a gap between two of the beams that was large enough for them to fit through.

"Blackcap, help me!" he whispered.

Blackcap hopped beneath the gap and Ragtag climbed on top of him. The swallow stuck his head through the hole, then quickly pulled back. The birds retreated a short distance.

"I saw them!" Ragtag whispered. "They're being held in a corner. The hole in the wood is unguarded. It's behind some boxes, and it seems that the raptors haven't discovered it!"

"Are the clan leaders okay?" Blackcap asked.

"They look shaken, but I don't think they're hurt."

"What do we do now?" one of Blackcap's brothers asked.

"We wait," Ragtag replied.

:::

Tattler, Headstrong, and a half-dozen other sparrows slipped into the trees across from the Old South Church. The birds quietly hopped from branch to branch, their mottled feathers helping them blend in with the foliage. They went as high as they dared before peeking out from behind the leaves.

Gunlad and three red-tailed hawks sat across the street on the roof of the Boston Public Library. Tattler's claws tightened. Hatred flooded through her as she thought of the friends she had lost at the river.

"Easy, Tattler," Headstrong whispered. "I know how you feel, but we have a job to do."

"I'm okay," Tattler replied.

"Do you think Ragtag's in position?"

Tattler looked at the church across the square and felt a pang of regret that she wasn't with him. She quickly buried the thought. Ragtag had his mission, and she had hers.

"I hope so," Tattler said. Inwardly she was worried. There were so many things that could go wrong. What if the window over the door wasn't open? What if they couldn't get into the attic? What if they were caught?

"Me too," Headstrong said, "because if he isn't, this is all going to be for nothing."

Tattler glanced at the raptors standing guard across the street.

"We've waited long enough," she whispered. "Tell the others to get ready."

Gunlad leaned over the edge of the roof to peer down on the square. He was bored. Bergelmir had ordered the hawks to keep watch for any sign of trouble, and they had been sitting restlessly for hours. Gunlad thought the emperor worried too much. After all, the Winged Regiment had been routed. If I were a sparrow, Gunlad thought, I'd be a hundred miles away by now.

A movement in the grass below caught his eye. One of the hawks launched himself from the roof. A moment later, he returned and laid the body of a mouse at his commander's feet. Gunlad glanced at the offering with disdain. He hated the food in the city. The mice were scrawny and tasted funny.

As soon as it was clear that Gunlad wasn't interested, the hawks pulled the mouse away and shared it among themselves. Gunlad sighed and turned his attention back to the square. He wished something would happen to break up the monotony of the day.

He didn't have long to wait. Shrill cries suddenly came from the trees opposite him. Gunlad and the hawks whirled around in surprise as eight sparrows zoomed across the street.

"Attack! Attack!" Tattler cried.

The three hawks fell back in shock as the sparrows rammed them head-on, their beaks snapping wildly.

Kittiwook

The Rescue

I nside the attic of the Old South Church, Bergelmir and the other raptors glanced up at the distant cries of the birds. Surt moved to the window and looked out.

"A band of sparrows is attacking Gunlad," the falcon reported. "Looks like a suicide."

"Make sure of it!" Bergelmir ordered.

"Hugin and Munin, come with me!"

The twin merlins followed the peregrine falcon out the window as Hoogol exchanged a glance with the clan leaders.

"What's going on?" Bobtail whispered.

"I'm not sure," Hoogol replied. "Sparrows are attacking the hawks."

"Are they insane?" Blue Feather asked. "They'll be killed for sure!"

"It's hopeless!" Bragi groaned.

As the birds talked nervously among themselves, nobody noticed Ragtag flutter up through the hole in the floor and take cover behind a crate. Blackcap and his brothers popped up behind him and looked around.

Bergelmir and Hod stood by the window, their attention focused outside. The clan leaders were in the opposite corner. Ragtag's spirits soared as he spotted Bobtail and Blue Feather standing next to Hoogol.

Quietly he hopped forward, trying to keep to the shadows as he made his way through the boxes scattered about the dusty attic. He took cover behind one and waved his wings to get their attention.

"*Pssst!*" Ragtag whispered. None of the hostages heard him. "*Pssst!*" he whispered more loudly.

Bobtail turned and caught sight of his brother. "I don't believe it," he said as he fell back in shock. "It's Rag—"

Ragtag motioned for him to keep quiet. Bobtail hopped over to Hoogol and whispered in his ear. The owl's massive head spun around, astonishment on his face as he spotted the young swallow.

Ragtag glanced at Bergelmir and Hod. The raptors still had their backs to him. He decided to risk it and flew over to the hostages. Hoogol immediately moved in front of him, his large bulk shielding the smaller bird from the raptors.

"Ragtag!" Blue Feather chirped.

"How did you get here?" Bobtail asked. "We thought you had run away!"

"Quiet, Bobtail," Hoogol said. "Let him talk."

"We've come to rescue you," Ragtag said.

"Rescue us?" Gini whispered. "How?"

"Tattler's outside causing a diversion. There's a hole in the floor at the back of the attic that leads into the rafters!"

"Watch out," Bobtail warned.

Ragtag quickly hid under one of the owl's wings as Bergelmir approached.

"Why are you whispering?" the osprey asked.

"We're wondering what's happening outside," Hoogol replied.

"A number of your sparrows are attacking my hawks," Bergelmir said. "But don't worry. Surt will make quick work of them."

Tattler and the sparrows darted about the birds of prey, careful to keep just out of reach of their beaks and talons.

"What's the matter, Gunlad?" Tattler taunted as she slipped away from him. "Too old and fat to catch me?"

"Stick around and find out, little girl," Gunlad snarled, chasing after her. Tattler laughed and reversed course with breathtaking speed.

"You and your hawks should go back to the country, where you belong!" Tattler yelled. "You don't have what it takes to catch us city birds."

"Keep playing with fire," Gunlad spat.

Tattler squawked as she lost a tail feather to the hawk's talons. She circled for another pass, determined to buy Ragtag more time.

"Heads up!" Headstrong yelled as he glanced over his shoulder and spotted Surt and the merlins zooming toward them. "Here come the reinforcements!"

A chill went through Tattler. Toying with hawks was one thing. A peregrine falcon was a different matter altogether.

"Retreat!" she yelled.

The sparrows broke off their attack and bolted south above the cars lining Boylston Street.

"Cheereek!"

The scream of a raptor echoed through the attic of the Old South Church. Ragtag peeked out from under Hoogol's wing and watched as Bergelmir and Hod whirled to face the window.

"What was that?" Bergelmir asked.

"It came from down in the square," Hod replied. "It sounded like an osprey."

"I know what it sounded like!" Bergelmir snapped. "Go and find out!"

Hod took flight and headed off to investigate as the other raptors crowded around the window. The clan leaders were forgotten for the moment.

"Now's our chance!" Ragtag whispered, and quietly led the birds to the hole in the floor.

"Get the pigeons out first," Hoogol said.

The pigeons adamantly shook their heads.

"We'll be caught," Bragi cried.

"Doomed! Doomed!" her flock softly cooed.

"Be quiet and go, or else Bergelmir will be the least of your troubles!" Hoogol hissed.

Bragi gulped and dropped through the hole. Ragtag stole a quick glance behind him. The birds of prey still had their backs turned.

"Come on!" Ragtag muttered as the pigeons followed their leader. Blackcap and his brothers had to jump on some of the fatter ones to get them through.

"Now the rest of you," Hoogol whispered.

One by one, the clan leaders escaped. Blue Feather was followed by Bobtail, then Gini. The starlings, swifts, and gulls went next. Three-quarters of the clan leaders were now in the rafters. Ragtag's spirits soared. *We just might make it,* he thought.

"Cheereek!" Kittiwook yelled again as she hopped back and forth under a bush near the Old South Church. The mockingbird was pleased with herself. She could imitate the call of any bird and took pride that her ability would play a vital role in rescuing Hoogol. A vision of the great horned owl praising her courage in front of the entire counsel sprang to mind. Like all mockingbirds, Kittiwook was a bit vain.

"Cheereek!" she yelled again. Unfortunately it never crossed her mind that her calls might do more than just distract the raptors.

Hod suddenly swooped down on her with open talons. The mockingbird squawked and took to the air, the kestrel pursuing her as she weaved through a crowd of humans.

Sensing that Hod had suddenly broken off the chase, Kittiwook landed on a park bench and turned to find the kestrel heading back to the attic.

"Hey!" she yelled, flapping her wings to draw his attention. "Where are you going? Come chase me!"

Hod didn't take the bait. He quickly flew back up to the window and landed next to Bergelmir.

"Well?" the osprey asked.

"It was a trick!" Hod gasped, struggling to catch his breath. "It was a mockingbird!"

"A mockingbird?" Bergelmir said thoughtfully. "But why would . . ."

He turned to see the last of the clan leaders escaping. Only Ragtag and Hoogol remained in the attic.

"Hoogol, hurry!" Ragtag yelled.

Hoogol tried to fit through the hole but Bergelmir covered the space separating them in a matter of seconds.

"It's no good," Hoogol said as the emperor slammed down in front of them. "Fly, Ragtag!"

Hoogol puffed up his feathers and faced the osprey while Hod went for Ragtag. The swallow managed to slip through the floorboards just before the kestrel reached him. Hod's hooked beak punched at the hole, trying in vain to enlarge it.

"Ragtag!" Hoogol's voice echoed through the rafters. "Get the others out!"

"I'm not leaving you," Ragtag called around Hod's snapping beak.

"There's nothing you can do for me! Now go, before it's too late!"

Ragtag hesitated as Bobtail and Blue Feather hopped forward.

"He's right," Bobtail said. "It's his fight now."

"Ragtag, please!" Blue Feather cried. "We don't know the way out."

Ragtag stared at the clan leaders and felt as if his heart were being torn in two. He knew he had no choice. "I'll come back for you, Hoogol," Ragtag yelled. Above them, the osprey and the owl continued to stare each other down. Hod gave up trying to enlarge the hole and returned to Bergelmir's side.

"Well?" Bergelmir demanded, never taking his eyes off Hoogol.

"They escaped," Hod replied.

"They have to come out somewhere. Take the hawks and find them."

Hod indicated Hoogol. "What about him?"

"I'll handle the owl," Bergelmir said. "Now go!"

The kestrel and the hawks departed as Bergelmir and Hoogol circled one another with raised wings.

"I should have done this the first time I laid eyes on you," Bergelmir snarled.

"You'll find, Bergelmir, that I'm not as tame as you think."

The two raptors launched themselves at each other and collided in the middle of the attic.

Hoogol and Bergelmir

T he clan leaders were scared, tired, and hungry. As Ragtag guided them through the endless rafters, he constantly had to stop and wait for them to catch up.

"Come on," he shouted. "Hurry!"

He was worried about Hoogol. Everything had gone so well up until the last moment. Why hadn't he realized that the hole in the floor would be too small for a great horned owl? The idea that they would all escape but that Hoogol was left behind to face Bergelmir alone was almost too much for him to handle.

"Hurry!" Ragtag yelled again as he emerged into the church. Below him, the human was still talking. The swallow soared across the chamber and landed on the railing of the pulpit, signaling the others to follow.

The human's voice trailed off as he spotted the motley band of birds flying over his head. Seagulls, pigeons, finches, blue jays, starlings, and more crossed the open space and joined their leader on the far side.

Ragtag turned and quickly fluttered down the circular staircase. Bobtail, Blue Feather, and the rest of the clan leaders followed him down the hall and up to the window. There was no sign of raptors.

"Bobtail," Ragtag said hurriedly, "take the clan leaders and head for the Common. Look for a pair of swans named Romeo and Juliet. They'll help you from there."

"Where are you going?"

"I've got to go back!"

"Ragtag, there's nothing you can do," Blue Feather said as she joined them on the windowsill. "This is a battle Hoogol has to fight alone. You'd just be in the way."

"I don't care," Ragtag said. "I have to try!" He flew past the startled birds and disappeared back up the staircase.

"How typical of my little brother," Bobtail fumed. "When we need him the most, he flies off on some fool's mission. I told you he'll never change, Mom. Ragtag's an unreliable, self-centered—"

"Enough! You're forgetting he just rescued us," Blue Feather said, then addressed the others. "We've got to go all at once. If we're pursued, split up and find the swans at the Common."

One by one, the birds flew out the window and emerged blinking into the bright light of day. They didn't have long to gain their bearings. Hod screamed as he plummeted toward them.

"Fly!" Blue Feather yelled.

It was everything Headstrong and the other sparrows could do to keep up with Tattler as she rocketed down Boylston

Street. The leader of the Winged Regiment was rumored to be one of the fastest birds in the city, and today she was proving those rumors to be true.

"It's no good," Headstrong yelled. "They're gaining on us!"

Tattler risked a glance behind her. Her stomach tightened as she saw Surt and the others closing the gap. "Scatter and draw some of them off."

Headstrong nodded. As the sparrows reached an intersection, they broke apart and darted away.

"I'll take the leader. Split up and follow the others!" Surt ordered. Gunlad, the hawks, and the twin merlins veered away as Surt followed Tattler down an alley.

A chill went through Tattler when she realized Surt was on her tail. Peregrine falcons were among the fastest birds in the sky. The sparrow forced herself to concentrate. She still had a few tricks to play. Tattler banked and headed for a building across the street. A human was exiting through a revolving glass door. She pumped her wings and flew inside. As she'd hoped, Surt entered the partition behind her.

The door whirled and the startled man jumped out. Tattler hovered in the air as the door made a complete turn. Just a little more, she thought. It began to slow and finally came to a stop, leaving a crack just wide enough for the sparrow to slip out and escape.

Surt tried to follow, but there was no opening in his partition. The peregrine falcon slammed himself against the glass over and over again.

In the church attic, Hoogol and Bergelmir were in a fight to the death. The two raptors clawed each other wildly as they parried to and fro. Normally an owl would be no match for an osprey, but Bergelmir was old and half blind. Hoogol pressed his advantage, forcing the osprey back against the wall.

"Do you remember when we first met?" Hoogol roared. "How you pledged your friendship to me? And then how you betrayed me? How you betrayed the nine? Your days of treachery are over!"

"I remember a foolish owl whose ego got the better of him." Bergelmir laughed. "Why fight me, Hoogol? Why not turn and run, like you did before? That's what you're best at, isn't it?"

Bergelmir's hooked beak bit deeply into Hoogol's flesh. The owl flapped his wings and shook the osprey off, then crashed into him. The two raptors rolled across the floor. Hoogol ended up on top, his talons digging into the osprey's flanks.

"You should have stayed in the country!" Hoogol said. "You're old and weak. Your days as emperor are at an end!"

"We shall see!" Bergelmir replied as he bit into Hoogol's wing, cutting down to the bone. Hoogol cried out and released his hold.

Bergelmir shook himself free. The two raptors scrambled back and regarded each other warily. Both had bare patches where their plumage had been ripped away. Their remaining feathers were covered in blood.

"You're getting tired," Bergelmir said. "I can sense it. You're going to die in this attic!"

The owl and the osprey hissed at each other as they continued to circle, each waiting for an opening.

"If my fate is to die here today," Hoogol panted, "so be it. But you'll die with me."

"Don't count on it," Bergelmir replied as both raptors lunged at each other. Hoogol suddenly lost his balance and toppled back. The osprey spotted his chance and pounced. The emperor's talons sank deep into Hoogol's chest.

"It's over, old fool," Bergelmir cackled. "Die, and know that the Feathered Alliance dies with you!"

Hoogol struggled to regain his footing, but the osprey's talons remained firmly embedded.

"The empire will never win!" Hoogol rasped. With a last burst of strength, the great horned owl picked the osprey up and flew forward.

The two raptors tumbled out the window and fell to the ledge along the outside of the church. Bergelmir landed on top of the owl. Desperately Hoogol tried to free himself, but the osprey's grasp was too strong.

Ragtag suddenly emerged through the hole in the floor and flew to the windowsill. He froze at the horrible sight in front of him. Hoogol lay helpless beneath the emperor. The owl's feathers were stained crimson, and his breathing was labored. Bergelmir laughed as his talons cut deeper into Hoogol's flesh.

"You and your pathetic city kind are no match for us," Bergelmir gloated. "I could kill you quickly, Hoogol, but I won't.

You were right when you said I take pleasure in the hunt. I want you to feel pain. I want to see you squirm like a rat. I want to hear the leader of the Feathered Alliance beg for mercy!"

Hoogol groaned as the osprey dug his talons in deeper.

"Beg for your life, Hoogol!"

"Never," the owl sobbed, his body wracked with pain as the osprey twisted his claws.

"You will very soon."

Something snapped inside Ragtag while he watched Hoogol struggling weakly beneath the osprey. Hatred flooded him as he listened to Bergelmir's laugh. The emperor had destroyed the city birds' way of life. He was going to enslave the clans. He was responsible for the death of Proud Beak and countless others. And now he was going to kill Hoogol.

Not if Ragtag could help it! His anger gave him strength, and he launched himself into the air, flapping his wings as hard as he could. "Bergelmir!" he screamed before ramming the leader of the Talon Empire with all his might.

Bergelmir was off balance when Ragtag collided with him. The already-weakened osprey lost his grip and his wings fluttered wildly as he fell off the ledge and plunged to the road below.

The osprey hit the pavement hard. He staggered to his feet and spread his wings to take flight but was distracted by a horn. Bergelmir whirled just as a car plowed into him.

The driver slammed on her brakes, and the vehicle skidded to a stop. An elderly human got out and hurried around to the front.

"Oh, no, what have I done?" she gasped as she saw the osprey under her wheel. "Don't die! Don't die! Oh, what have I done?"

She tried to prop up Bergelmir, but the osprey's broken and lifeless body flopped back down to the pavement.

High above the street, Ragtag watched in shock. "I don't believe it," he said. "I killed Bergelmir. I killed the emperor."

A groan broke into his thoughts. Ragtag quickly hurried back to Hoogol. The owl was in bad shape.

"Ragtag," Hoogol said weakly. "Bergelmir, is he . . ."

"Bergelmir's dead," Ragtag replied. "The emperor's dead."

He glanced up at the sky. "Hoogol, we've got to get out of here! It's only a matter of time until the other raptors return."

Hoogol tried to raise himself, then fell back. "I can't," the owl said. "Save yourself, Ragtag. Fly before the hawks return."

"No! I'm not going to let you die. Get up, Hoogol!"

Ragtag hopped over to the owl and pushed his beak against him.

"It's no use," the owl said. "I can't make it."

"Yes, you can! Now get up!"

Hoogol made a supreme effort and climbed to his feet.

"Just spread your wings and glide," Ragtag said. "The wind will carry you."

The owl shakily spread his wings.

"Jump, Hoogol," Ragtag encouraged. "I'll be right behind you."

Hoogol fell off the ledge and glided down to Boylston Street. The owl landed hard on the sidewalk and fell on his face. Ragtag fluttered down beside him and pulled on the owl's wing with his beak. "Come on, Hoogol! We can't stay here."

Humans had already spotted them and were beginning to form a crowd. Ragtag redoubled his efforts to drag Hoogol to safety. The great horned owl finally managed to get to his feet, and the two birds crawled off beneath a tree.

A group of people had gathered behind the revolving door in the lobby of the office building where Surt was trapped. They watched the peregrine with a mixture of curiosity and amusement as he loudly protested his imprisonment.

A little girl clutched at her father. "Can I keep him, Daddy? He's sooooo cute! Please?"

The man looked uncertainly at the large bird. "I don't think so. He belongs in the wild. Besides, he doesn't seem very friendly."

The unintelligible sounds made by the humans were driving Surt mad. He fluttered into the air and threw himself against the glass.

"I'll give him credit for one thing," the girl's father said as he pulled her away. "He's certainly persistent."

The humans laughed at the raptor's attempts to free himself. But their laughter came to a sudden stop when Surt cracked the glass.

The father rushed forward and pushed the revolving door, dumping the falcon unceremoniously onto the sidewalk. Surt jumped to his feet and shook his wings at the humans standing behind the glass.

"Fools!" he screamed. Hissing one last time at the crowd, he took to the air and headed back to Copley Square.

Gunlad, Hod, and the assembled hawks sat quietly on the roof of the Old South Church. Their attention was focused on the street below, so they didn't notice when Surt landed next to them. The falcon quickly hopped into the attic, found it empty, and returned.

"Where's Hoogol?" Surt snapped. "Where are the clan leaders?"

"They escaped," Gunlad said in a daze.

"Escaped? How?" The falcon glanced around him. "Where's Bergelmir?"

Hod indicated the street below. Surt dropped off the roof and flew down to the top of a lamp. His beak fell open in shock. Beneath him, two humans were shoveling the osprey into a trash bag.

Surt

The Falcon Emperor

R agtag helped Hoogol crawl beneath a Dumpster. The wind had blown a pile of leaves into one corner. The great horned owl collapsed onto the makeshift bed, his breath ragged.

"We can hide here until nightfall," Ragtag said, peering out at the alley. From his vantage point, he could see a small section of Copley Square. Birds of prey were still circling over the church.

Hoogol coughed wretchedly. "I'm afraid I may not live that long."

"Don't talk like that!" Ragtag said, and hopped back to the wounded owl. "Of course you're going to live. We need you, Hoogol. With Proud Beak gone, you're our only hope."

Hoogol gazed fondly at the swallow. "It wasn't me who killed Bergelmir."

"I just pushed him off a ledge," Ragtag said. "He would never have fallen if he hadn't been so weak from fighting you. Promise me you won't die, Hoogol."

"I only make promises I can keep," Hoogol said. Then he added quickly, "But I'll try my best."

"This is all Loki's fault," Ragtag muttered. "If it weren't for him, the clan leaders would've been able to flee in time."

"I feel no anger toward him," Hoogol said as he coughed again and began to shiver. "Indeed, I feel mostly pity."

"Pity?"

"Loki is young and foolish, and has made a great mistake. In time, he will come to see the error of his ways."

"You give him too much credit."

"I believe all of us can be redeemed."

"I don't see how. To make a pact with a monster like Bergelmir is unthinkable. He has no conscience. He doesn't care about anyone except himself!"

The great horned owl looked sad. "That may be so," Hoogol said quietly. "But I know of another who made a pact with Bergelmir and lived to see the error of his ways."

"Who?" Ragtag asked.

"A young owl named Hoogol."

"No! I don't believe it. You would never have betrayed the Feathered Alliance. You're nothing like Loki!"

"I would not have sacrificed one clan of birds to save another," Hoogol said. "But like Loki, I was misled by the inexperience of youth. I allowed my ego and pride to get the better of me. Like Loki, I believed the birds of prey would honor their words. Unfortunately I believe it's only a matter of time until he learns the same lesson I did."

Ragtag hopped closer. Even though he knew he shouldn't tax the old owl's strength, he was spellbound. Hoogol had always been a revered and mysterious figure, glimpsed only now and then from a distance as he presided over the meetings in the belfry.

"A long time ago," Hoogol said, "there was a stretch of pristine woods far from here. It was the woods where I was born. There were no humans there back then. The forest was vast and deep, and it provided shelter and comfort to a great many clans.

"The birds of those woods lived in peace, and were governed by a high council of nine owls. These were the oldest and wisest of those inhabiting the woods, and they settled disputes with fairness and compassion."

"Just like the Feathered Alliance," Ragtag chirped.

"Indeed, just like our alliance," Hoogol said. "The nine owls were respected far and wide, and I was very proud that my own father sat among them. You might find this hard to believe, but back then I was as young and impetuous, not to mention irresponsible, as a certain young swallow I know."

Ragtag cringed and looked down.

"I was also as ambitious and stubborn as another swallow we both know."

"Bobtail!" Ragtag exclaimed.

"Yes, Bobtail," Hoogol said. "Like your brother, I desperately wanted to prove myself. It was my dream that one day I would sit among the nine. It was this dream that blinded me, that led me to make the greatest mistake of my life. It began with the coming of Fenrir."

Hoogol's eyes clouded over as his thoughts drifted to the past. "One day a great storm fell upon the woodlands. And with it came the Talon Empire. They came from the north, driven by their search for food. The woods I lived in had food enough for all, and I'm sure that if they had come in peace, they would have been welcomed. But it was not the way of Fenrir to share."

"Fenrir?" Ragtag asked in a hushed voice.

"Fenrir was the father of Bergelmir," Hoogol explained. "He was a vicious osprey, stronger and more powerful even than Surt. He ordered his troops to mass for an attack against our woods in much the same way the birds of prey have now attacked our city."

Hoogol coughed again, and Ragtag hopped forward. "Please don't talk any more, Hoogol. Save your strength."

Hoogol shook his head. "For so long I have kept this secret to myself. I want you to know, Ragtag. It's a relief to finally tell someone."

Ragtag sat down and Hoogol continued. "As I said earlier, I was young and foolish. Like Loki, I didn't understand the nature of evil. While both sides prepared for war, I was convinced there was another way.

"I thought I had discovered it when out hunting one day at the edge of the woods. I ran across a young scout from the empire. He was alone, having lost his way."

"Bergelmir," Ragtag said.

"Yes," Hoogol replied, "but it was not the Bergelmir of today. He was little more than a fledgling then, and I believed he had an open heart. I saw him as much like me, a bird wanting desperately to prove himself in the eyes of his father.

"I forged a friendship with Bergelmir and guided him back to where the birds of prey were camped. Bergelmir convinced me that his father could be persuaded to seek peace, and that the Talon Empire and the clans of the woods could live together. He persuaded me to meet his father, which I did. Fenrir told me that he, too, desired peace, and offered to go alone with me to the owls to plead his cause.

"It was then that I made my greatest mistake. Blinded by my own ego, I led Fenrir and Bergelmir to the secret grotto where the nine held council. The only thoughts that filled my head were of how great a hero I would be in the eyes of my father. I underestimated the treachery of the empire and paid for it dearly."

"What happened?" Ragtag asked.

"I was betrayed," Hoogol replied. "Bergelmir and his father had no desire for peace and used me to accomplish their real goal. I thought I was leading them alone through the woods. Little did I know that accipiters were shadowing us, and the entire empire was on the move.

"When we arrived at the grotto, Fenrir confronted the Council of Nine and, to my horror, demanded they bow to him. The owls, including my father, refused. Without warning, we were attacked from above by an army of hawks."

Hoogol closed his eyes. "I remember the screams and cries as the nine were slaughtered. I remember my own father gasping as he was cut down. I remember the look in his eyes. It was the look of a father gazing upon a son who had betrayed him."

Hoogol's voice grew hoarse. "My father died that day,

along with the others. He died thinking I had betrayed him to the empire."

Ragtag averted his eyes in anguish. "But you couldn't have known," he cried. "It wasn't your fault. It was Bergelmir's!"

Hoogol sank back in exhaustion. "It was my fault. I was taught a lesson that day, a lesson about the perils of pride, about what can happen if you put thoughts of yourself over thoughts of others."

"What happened next?" Ragtag asked.

"I turned to face Bergelmir, only to discover him laughing at me. Where before he had seemed kind and open, he now seemed cruel and full of hate. To my shame, I fled the grotto. The Talon Empire routed the clans of the woods. They scattered and many were lost. I myself traveled alone, consumed with guilt, until one day I happened upon this city. The rest I believe you already know. The seagulls adopted me as their own, and I was only too eager to put the horrors of the past behind me.

"For years, I tried not to think of the empire or of the mistakes I had made. In time, I grew old, as did Bergelmir. Fenrir died, and Bergelmir assumed the throne. So, too, I came into my own, as the leader of the Feathered Alliance.

"For all these years, the thought that the empire would one day march upon the city was always at the back of my mind. But as time passed and there was no sign, I grew complacent. I reasoned that the great woods of the west would satisfy Bergelmir and his kind. I didn't foresee that the humans would one day drive them from it."

"I'm just glad Bergelmir's dead," Ragtag said. "At least it's finally over."

"I wish it were that easy," Hoogol replied.

"What do you mean?"

"The Talon Empire is more than just one ruler. As Bergelmir assumed the throne from Fenrir, so now will Bergelmir's heir be crowned."

"Surt," Ragtag said with a sinking heart.

Night fell upon the city. More than two dozen raptors had gathered in the attic of the Old South Church as word of Bergelmir's death spread like wildfire. They bowed their heads as Surt stalked back and forth. The peregrine falcon was in a horrible mood. Nobody wanted to address him. Finally Gunlad stepped forward.

"My lord, there is the matter of succession. With Bergelmir gone—"

Surt whirled, his beady eyes filled with rage. The hawk looked away, and the falcon continued to pace.

"With Bergelmir gone," Gunlad continued after clearing his throat, "you are now emperor. We all pledge our loyalty."

The raptors hailed their new leader. Surt didn't seem to care much about his new rank. He loomed over the raptors. "Who killed Bergelmir?"

The hawks averted their eyes. Nobody dared respond.

"I asked a question!" Surt snarled. "You're telling me nobody knows? Why was nobody here?"

Hod stepped forward. "Bergelmir ordered me to pursue the clan leaders. He said he wanted to deal with Hoogol himself."

"And did you catch them?"

The kestrel nervously shifted his weight. "I'm sorry, m'lord. They escaped."

"Weakling!" Surt roared, and struck Hod with one of his talons. The kestrel stumbled back, his face bleeding.

"Let that be a lesson," Surt hissed. "The next time you fail me, you won't escape with a mere scratch."

"Yes, m'lord," Hod muttered, and backed away.

"What happened to Bergelmir?" Surt yelled as he turned to the others. "Do you really expect me to believe that an old owl killed the ruler of the Talon Empire?"

A familiar voice suddenly rang out from the far side of the attic. "It wasn't Hoogol who killed Bergelmir."

Surt and the other raptors watched as Loki emerged from the shadows. "I saw the whole thing from a tree," the crow said. "Bergelmir and Hoogol were locked in a fight to the death. The osprey would have won, had he not been pushed to his death."

"Pushed by whom?" Surt demanded. Loki hesitated, and Surt took a menacing stop forward. "Answer me! Pushed by whom?"

"By a young swallow," Loki said quietly, "named Ragtag."

The raptors squawked among themselves.

"Quiet!" Surt roared, then loomed over the crow. "You're telling me that a swallow killed an osprey?"

"That's exactly what I'm telling you."

"And what of Hoogol?"

"Hoogol no longer matters. The owl is either dead or will be soon. Bergelmir saw to that."

Surt shook with rage as he faced his troops. "I swear to you that Bergelmir shall be avenged. Find this Ragtag! If you have to kill every bird in the city, do it. But bring him to me alive!" Half the raptors departed at once.

"As for the rest of these miserable creatures, destroy them!" Surt continued. "Wipe the Feathered Alliance from the sky. Show no mercy to those who killed our leader!"

Loki cautiously hopped forward and bowed before the falcon.

"Please remember, my lord, that the crows are to be spared."

Surt whirled on him. "The crows will not be spared! They are traitors, liars, and thieves. They will be treated as such!"

"The crows were to remain free!" Loki protested. "That was the agreement I made with Bergelmir."

"Bergelmir is no longer emperor," Surt hissed. "And I'm changing the agreement. Be thankful I don't rip you to shreds!"

Loki was wise enough not to respond. He bowed low and quickly retreated into the shadows.

Hoogol lay on a bed of moss beneath the bridge in the Public Garden. The owl's eyes were closed, and he was breathing with difficulty. Surrounding him were the clan leaders whom Ragtag had rescued from Bergelmir's lair.

Hoogol shifted on the moss, and the birds started. The great horned owl said something unintelligible and fell back into a restless sleep. Tattler got to her feet and left the circle.

Ragtag stood a short distance away. A fog bank had rolled

in over the city, blocking any raptor's view from above. It was a welcome relief, but he knew it wouldn't last.

He watched as the swans glided in and out of the mist hanging over the lake. The birds of prey had left them alone. Perhaps the empire had realized that swans were under the protection of the humans. Ragtag felt a burst of jealousy. Why couldn't the humans protect them all?

The swallow turned and stared at Hoogol. Under the cover of the fog, Ragtag had managed to get the great horned owl to the safety of the Common. It had been a long and arduous journey, and at times he'd thought Hoogol wouldn't make it. The owl's left wing was broken and trailed along on the ground behind him. He had a deep wound in his chest and was coughing up blood.

"Hoogol's dying," Tattler said as she joined Ragtag. "I'm afraid he won't last the night."

A wave of despair washed over him. "I did everything I could!"

"I know you did. You can't blame yourself. It's not your fault. If it weren't for you, he wouldn't have lasted this long."

Ragtag looked away. "I just wish I could have done more. Sometimes I feel cursed that I was born a swallow. I'm so small and useless."

Tattler's face hardened with determination. "And yet it was you who brought down the ruler of the Talon Empire. I'd say that's not a bad achievement for a young swallow."

"But at what cost?" Ragtag said as he glanced at the great horned owl.

Headstrong suddenly flew in under the bridge and

landed next to them. His feathers were askew, and Ragtag noticed that several were missing from his tail.

"You okay?" Tattler asked.

"Had a run-in . . . with a pair . . . of merlins," Headstrong gasped.

"Hugin and Munin?"

"They're the ones. Vicious girls. One of them almost got me, but I managed to escape unscathed." Headstrong glanced at his tail. "Well, almost. I hope they grow back."

The other birds surrounded the trio and demanded whatever news Headstrong could provide. The sparrow took a quick drink from the lake, then gave his report. "It's not good. The raptors have gone wild. Surt's furious about the death of Bergelmir. By the way, he's been proclaimed their new emperor."

The clan leaders exchanged worried looks.

"It gets worse," Headstrong continued. "Surt knows Ragtag was involved."

"How could he?" Tattler asked. "I left him trapped!"

"I don't know, but he does. He's ordered the raptors to round up all the swallows in the city." Headstrong glanced at Ragtag. "I'd keep a low profile if I were you. He's out for blood."

Ragtag felt a chill go down his spine.

"Surt has gone crazy," Headstrong continued. "The raptors are destroying our nests, taking our eggs, and killing any who oppose them. The clans are being wiped out."

"What good is killing Bergelmir when Surt simply takes his place?" Gini chirped. "If anything, Surt's more powerful!"

"I hate to say this," Bobtail said loudly, "but Gini's right. Ragtag may have done more harm than good by killing that osprey." The clan leaders erupted in a chorus of agreement.

Tattler hopped forward to defend Ragtag. "That's ludicrous, Bobtail, and you know it!"

"Yeah," Blackcap added in a high-pitched voice. "You're just jealous!"

"Jealous?" Bobtail repeated with an air of indignation. "Jealous of what?"

"Of your little brother!" the chickadee shot back. "Of the fact that he single-handedly killed the emperor and rescued all of you when you were helpless."

Blackcap glared at Gini. "You seem to be forgetting that. Or perhaps you'd rather be back in that attic?"

The starling's beak opened and closed, but no words emerged.

"Enough of this bickering!" Hoogol rasped from behind them. The great horned owl made a mighty effort and raised himself from the moss.

"Listen to what I have to say, while there's still time."

The birds crowded around their leader. Hoogol's eyes seemed distant, and he coughed deeply before continuing.

"Ragtag, come closer," the owl rasped. Ragtag slowly hopped forward. "Your actions tonight were great and courageous. I made a mistake in banishing you. I want to apologize while I still can, and also to thank you."

"Hoogol, you don't have to—"

"No, I must. You gave me a special gift. You gave me the opportunity to die here, surrounded by my friends . . . instead of in that foul creature's grasp. And I can die at peace, knowing that my death and my father's death have already been avenged."

Ragtag bowed his head, overcome with grief as the great horned owl made one last effort to lift himself farther. He raised his head from the moss and gazed fondly at the assembled birds.

"My friends," Hoogol said, his voice unsteady and labored. "I know I won't be with you for the battles that lie ahead. And yet I still have hope that you will somehow emerge victorious. Ragtag has shown that it's not the size of one's beak or claw that will win this war, but the size of one's heart."

The old owl lay back down and smiled weakly at Ragtag. "I believe this young swallow to be the future of the Feathered Alliance. . . ."

And with that, Hoogol closed his eyes forever.

Gini

A Symbol of Hope

L oki flew as fast as he dared through the fog. He had been stuck in the attic of the Old South Church for hours, waiting for the raptors to fall asleep. Finally Hugin and Munin had nodded off and he had managed to tiptoe past them and out the window.

The crow cursed his luck. After his spies had reported the death of Bergelmir, he had decided to gamble and betray the birds of the city even further. He had hoped to gain Surt's favor by telling him about Ragtag, but instead he had suffered the falcon's wrath.

I had no choice, Loki thought. I did what I had to do to protect the crows. Ragtag would have done the same had he been in my position.

The crow shook off his feelings of guilt and followed a set of train tracks north. The fog was making flying almost impossible, and more than once, he lost sight of the ground and panicked as he was enveloped in the mist.

Finally he saw the lights of South Station ahead of him, but instinctively he knew something was wrong. A disheartening quiet lay upon the train yard. No sentries rose to challenge him. Loki beat his wings harder as the abandoned locomotive that served as the crows' meeting place loomed out of the fog.

"No!" he screamed. His worst fears had come true: The ground was littered with the bodies of dead crows. He landed and hopped forward. Signs of a great fight could be seen all around him.

Loki walked through the yard in a daze. He finally stopped when he found what he was looking for. The bodies of his younger brothers, Fafnir and Gungmir, lay next to each other on the bloodied ground. The crow staggered back, overcome with grief.

A rustling came from beneath the locomotive. Loki crossed over to investigate. The dark shape of another bird suddenly leaped out and knocked him to the ground. The two rolled end over end in a mass of snapping beaks and scratching claws.

Loki finally managed to break free and whirled to face his attacker. "Garm!"

Garm stopped as he recognized his leader. "Loki! I—I'm sorry. I thought you were one of them."

"Garm, what happened? Who did this?"

"Sharpies," Garm muttered.

Loki felt a chill go down his spine. Sharp-shinned hawks were notorious for their brutality.

"A band of them attacked us without reason," Garm continued. "They slaughtered us for sport! Loki, it was horrible. They were laughing. It was nothing but a game to them. We tried to rally a defense, but . . ."

"Easy, Garm. They're gone now."

Loki helped the old crow to the ground. Garm was badly injured. His face was slashed, one eye was swollen shut, and blood stained his feathers.

"Loki, I'm sorry," Garm said. "Fafnir and Gungmir . . ."

"I know," Loki replied. "I found them. Did anyone survive?"

"A few, but they were rounded up and taken away. What happened? The agreement—"

"The agreement's been broken. Surt betrayed us. The crows are now fair game for the raptors, along with everyone else."

"What are we going to do?"

"Can you fly?"

"I think so."

"Then find as many crows as you can and tell them to go into hiding. They're not to attack the empire. They wouldn't stand a chance."

"Loki—"

"I brought this curse upon us," Loki said, "and it's my responsibility alone to deal with it."

"But how? What are you going to do?"

Loki gazed at the bodies of his two brothers. Finally he said, "I'll do what must be done."

Hoogol's body lay on a nest of twigs and branches that had been placed on the lake in the Public Garden. The clan leaders watched somberly as the swans pushed it out into the water. The nest drifted away and vanished into the fog.

For a long moment, nobody spoke and nothing could be heard except for Blue Feather's sobs and the muted cooing of the pigeons. Then the birds turned and made their way back beneath the bridge. They didn't have much time to mourn. A magpie hopped forward and shook her wings in a panic.

"What are we going to do? Both Hoogol and Proud Beak are gone!"

"We need a new leader," Gini said.

Bobtail eagerly hopped forward. "I've spent the most time with the council. I've worked with Proud Beak. I know how to run the alliance better than anyone."

"That's fine and good," Headstrong snapped. "But with all due respect, we don't need a politician. We need a *real* leader."

Bobtail's face flushed.

"But who?" Bragi cried.

"Who? Who?" the pigeons cooed.

"Tattler should be our leader," Headstrong declared. "She's the commander of the Winged Regiment. There's nobody more qualified to lead us in a time of war."

There was a chorus of agreement. Tattler shook her head. "Not me. I have my wings full with the sparrows. I think it should be Ragtag."

"What?" Bobtail exploded. "Why, just because he happened to be in the right place at the right time to knock an old osprey off a ledge? You call that leadership?"

"Hoogol said Ragtag was the future of the Feathered Alliance."

"What's that supposed to mean?"

"Bobtail's right," Gini said. "Hoogol never said that Ragtag should be our leader, just that he was the future. I think he was a bit delirious toward the end, anyway."

"Ragtag freed the hostages and killed Bergelmir!" Blackcap piped up. "If any bird can rally and inspire the clans to fight, it's him."

"Yes," Bragi said. "Let's elect Ragtag."

"Ragtag! Ragtag!" the pigeons chanted.

Bobtail desperately flapped his wings for attention. "Listen to me, everyone! Ragtag's my brother and all, but as a leader . . ."

The birds paid Bobtail no attention and crowded around Ragtag.

"Ragtag! Ragtag! Ragtag!" the clan leaders all yelled in unison.

"Well, Ragtag?" Headstrong asked.

Ragtag had a bewildered look on his face. "But . . . I'm just a swallow. I don't know anything about fighting a war or leading an alliance."

Tattler hopped to his side. "That's why you'll have Headstrong and me to advise you."

The birds waited apprehensively for Ragtag's answer. Ragtag gaped at the crowd. Finally Blue Feather hopped forward. "Ragtag, can I see you in private?"

"Phew, that was close," Bobtail said as he watched Ragtag hop off with their mother. "She'll talk him out of it."

Blue Feather waited until they were out of earshot of the others, then faced her younger son. "I didn't get a chance to thank you for rescuing us. I always knew there was more to you than meets the eye."

"Mom, I can't lead the alliance!"

"Why not?"

"Because I'm just . . . Ragtag. Hoogol and Proud Beak, they were both warriors and great leaders. I'm nothing like that."

"Do you really believe great leaders are born?" Blue Feather asked. "Do you think Hoogol was great and wise when he first accepted the leadership of the alliance? As I recall, he wasn't much older than you are now."

Ragtag didn't respond. He was thinking of what Hoogol had told him, of the mistakes he had made in trusting Bergelmir, and how he'd had to learn the hard way how to be a great leader.

"But it was just dumb luck that I was the one who killed the emperor," Ragtag said. "I'm nothing more than a symbol."

"Exactly," Blue Feather replied. "A powerful symbol. Do you think the clan leaders want you because of your strength? Or because you're the fastest bird in the air, or have the sharpest claws? They certainly don't want your brother, and heaven knows he can run a council meeting better than any of us. They want you, Ragtag, exactly *because* you're a symbol. Whoever would have thought that a young swallow could have brought down the ruler of the Talon Empire?"

Ragtag shook his head and stared at the birds watching him anxiously from under the bridge.

"The clans will rally around you," Blue Feather continued. "They'll be inspired by you. They see in you a chance to accomplish the impossible, a chance to actually win. I hope you won't let them down."

Tattler, Headstrong, and the others waited as Ragtag and Blue Feather made their way back to them.

"Well?" Blackcap asked.

Ragtag took a deep breath. "I don't know how good I'll be, but if you really want me, I guess I'm willing to give it a shot. So . . . I accept!"

A great cheer rose into the air. It wasn't unanimous. Gini shook her head and whispered about how foolish and inexperienced a leader Ragtag would make. And Bobtail flew into the fog muttering to himself.

Blue Feather winked at Ragtag as the other clan leaders surrounded him.

"Ragtag, what are we going to do?" Bragi cried. "How can we fight the raptors?"

All eyes turned to Ragtag. He realized that he had to say something, and fast. He looked at Tattler. "Is it possible to rally the Winged Regiment? To get the sparrows back together?"

"It would take some time," Tattler said. "And it would be dangerous, but I suppose anything's possible. The question is, why would you want to? We already fought the raptors once, and it was a disaster. We'd lose if we faced them again."

"Not if we had some help . . ." Ragtag said.

Bragi shook her wings. "What bird can fight a peregrine falcon and win?"

"I know of only one bird who can defeat Surt," Ragtag declared. "And his name is Baldur!"

Stunned silence filled the air. The birds stared at Ragtag.

"You mean to tell us your story about that eagle was true?" Headstrong asked.

"Of course it was true," Ragtag replied, slightly annoyed. "I helped free him and he gave me his promise that he would come to my aid if I ever asked. I don't know what happened to him that night, but he made a promise. And eagles don't break their promises—or so I've been told."

"But, Ragtag," Tattler said, "if Baldur really does exist, where is he?"

"I don't know," Ragtag admitted. "That's what we have to find out. And fast!"

A familiar voice suddenly piped up from behind them. "I know where your eagle is."

The surprised birds turned to see Loki flap down from the branch where he had been spying on them.

"Traitor!" Tattler screamed. Before the crow could react, both Tattler and Headstrong plowed into him. Loki squawked as claws tore at his feathers and beaks slashed at his wings.

"Wait!" Ragtag cried. "Get off him!"

"Ragtag, no!" Gini protested. "He'll kill us all!"

Ragtag hopped over and pecked at Tattler. "If I'm to be the leader of the Feathered Alliance, you'll have to follow my orders. Now get off him! I want to hear what he has to say."

Tattler, Headstrong, and the others reluctantly hopped back as Loki slowly crawled to his feet.

"Congratulations on your new rank, Ragtag," Loki muttered. "Although it has to be said, your hospitality is worse than Hoogol's."

"You should thank me for not letting them kill you,"

Ragtag replied. "After the way you betrayed us, heaven knows I should."

"I did what I thought was right at the time!" Loki cried. "I acted to save the crows."

"You saved your own clan at the expense of all the others!" Tattler yelled. "Ragtag, this crow is the reason Hoogol and Proud Beak are dead. He's lied to us again and again. Don't listen to whatever he has to say. Take my advice and kill him now!"

Ragtag didn't respond.

The crow looked around nervously as the other birds formed a circle and slowly closed in. "I'm not here to give excuses!" Loki squeaked. "I made a mistake and I've paid the price! Surt slaughtered my brethren. He killed my brothers. The crows have been enslaved along with the rest of the clans."

"Good," said Tattler. "It's a fitting justice."

Loki ignored her and faced Ragtag. "I know you don't want to hear an apology, so I won't give you one. I can only try to make amends."

Bobtail fluttered to a landing under the bridge. He had heard the commotion and hurried back. "Ragtag, you're a fool if you listen to him! He'll betray us again."

"If I were going to turn you in to the emperor," Loki replied, "I would simply have led his raptors here." The crow turned to Ragtag. "As I said, the crows are no longer free. We may not like each other, but I can help you destroy the empire. It's in my own interest to do so."

"What do you know of Baldur?" Ragtag asked.

"Crows may be poor and outcast, but our spies are everywhere. You think you were alone when you freed that eagle? You weren't. The crows were watching. We were watching when you returned to the belfry to tell Hoogol about Baldur, and we were watching when the humans came after you left and captured him!"

Ragtag's beak fell open. "The humans with their lights, searching the riverbank during the storm!"

"Yes," Loki replied. "They arrived as soon as you left."

"You know where Baldur is being held?"

"He's far from here, but not far enough to be unknown to the crows. He's being held by the humans in one of their buildings on the other side of the Great Water."

"Why?"

Loki shrugged. "Humans often meddle in the affairs of others. They catch eagles, release them, sometimes even keep them for their entire lives. I don't know why, but I can take you to him if you wish."

Tattler nudged Ragtag. He followed her until they were out of earshot of the others.

"Tattler, I know why you hate crows," Ragtag began.

"This has nothing to do with that," Tattler snapped. "This is about common sense, plain and simple. A crow would never willingly help us, especially not this one."

"Not unless it's in his own interest. But if what he says is true, then Surt broke Bergelmir's agreement. The crows are as bad off as we are."

"Ragtag, I think you're making a terrible mistake."

Ragtag glanced at Loki, who was anxiously awaiting his decision. "Perhaps I am. And you're right, Loki alone is responsible for Hoogol's death. But I can't help thinking of something Hoogol told me. He said Loki wasn't evil, just misguided."

Tattler shook her head. "Hoogol was old and far too trusting. He should never have allowed that accursed crow to leave the belfry in the first place!"

"Maybe," Ragtag said. "But Hoogol himself made a great mistake when he was young, and he redeemed himself. I think he would've wanted Loki to be given the same chance."

Tattler shook her wings in frustration. "This is madness. But you're right about one thing: If you're to be the leader of the Feathered Alliance, I'll have to start abiding by your decisions."

"Thanks, Tattler."

The two birds flew back to the others. Ragtag took a deep breath and declared, "I've made up my mind. I'm going to accept Loki's offer and let him guide me to Baldur."

Instantly there were squawks of alarm.

"No, Ragtag, no!" Bragi shouted. "Don't trust him!"

"This is how you lead the Feathered Alliance?" Gini yelled. "By turning us over to the one who betrayed us?"

"I have no choice but to trust him," Ragtag said. "None of us has any choice! Without the eagle, we can't fight Surt. Without Baldur, we're as good as dead. Tattler, I want you to take command until I return."

"No way! That's one order I won't obey. If you're going on this fool's quest, then I'm going with you." Tattler glared at the crow. "Somebody's got to keep an eye on your back with him around!"

Bobtail sat by himself at the edge of the lake, watching as the swans floated by. It was late, and the other birds were deep in preparations for Ragtag's departure. Bobtail couldn't bear to be there. His entire life had been dedicated to the council, to Proud Beak and Hoogol, to the alliance itself. How many days had he spent working while Ragtag flew off to play? Now his little brother was to be the leader of the Feathered Alliance?

Ragtag suddenly landed next to him. No doubt he's come to gloat, Bobtail thought. For a long moment, neither spoke. Finally Bobtail couldn't take it anymore.

"It's not fair!" Bobtail exploded. "I'm the oldest. I should have been the one who killed Bergelmir, the one who got elected leader!"

Ragtag winced. "I'm sorry, Bobtail. I didn't plan any of this."

Bobtail muttered something that Ragtag couldn't make out. Ragtag hopped closer. "Bobtail, I need your help. I need my brother's help! You have to take command of the Feathered Alliance while I'm gone. There's nobody better qualified to lead it."

"You can say that again."

"So you'll do it?"

"But I don't know how to be a leader," Bobtail said sarcastically. "I'm not a great big osprey-killing warrior like you."

"Stop being silly!"

"What about Headstrong? No doubt he'll want to take command now that Tattler's going with you."

"Headstrong's a soldier. He'll follow whatever orders Tattler gives him." Ragtag hopped closer. "Bobtail, you have to rally the sparrows while I'm gone."

Bobtail gave his brother a withering look. "If the sparrows regroup," he said in a condescending tone, "Surt will learn of it. We'll lose the element of surprise."

Ragtag hadn't thought of that. He glanced up at the sky. "Then we'll coordinate the attack. Let it be at noon the day after the next full moon."

"But that's in two days!"

"Loki thinks it'll be enough time for us to find Baldur and return."

Bobtail didn't respond. Ragtag stared at him, a pleading look in his eyes. "Bobtail, please . . ."

Finally Bobtail gave in. "Okay, I'll do it. For our mother's sake, if nothing else."

"Thanks," Ragtag said. "I knew I could count on you."

"Just remember one thing, Ragtag: If I do as you ask—if the sparrows attack—and there's no eagle, it will be the end of us all."

Hugin & Munin

The Quest Begins

It was early in the morning and still dark when the clan leaders gathered under the bridge one last time to see Ragtag, Tattler, and Loki off. Ragtag crossed over to say goodbye to his brother.

"Best of luck," Ragtag said.

"You too," Bobtail replied curtly and flew off.

He watched as his mother said her farewells to Tattler. When she caught sight of him, she hurried over. Blue Feather, who had seemed so calm and collected before, began to tremble as she embraced her son for what they both knew might be the last time.

"Are you going to be okay?" Ragtag asked.

"Don't worry about me," Blue Feather replied. "You just look after yourself." She hesitated, then asked, "Are you sure you really have to go?"

"You're the one who talked me into this," Ragtag reminded her. "You know, all that stuff about being a symbol?"

"I know, I know, but before I was talking with my head.

Now I'm talking with my heart." She placed a wing over her son and held him tightly. "Promise me you won't trust that crow!"

"Don't worry. That's one promise I'll keep."

"At least Tattler will be with you," Blue Feather said. "She'll get you through this. My poor little Ragtag, who's never even been out of the city before. What's to become of you? What's to become of us all?"

Ragtag struggled to break free of his mother's embrace. The other birds were beginning to stare.

"Mom, please," Ragtag whispered. "This is embarrassing."

"Sorry." Blue Feather sniffed and reluctantly let go. She watched as Ragtag hopped away to get some last-minute advice from the other elders. She was amazed at how much he had changed in these past few days. She was proud he was becoming everything she had known he could be. At the same time, a deep misgiving was growing inside her. She knew the dangers he would soon be facing, and a part of her wished that he were once again a carefree swallow who would rather ride the wind than shoulder any real responsibility.

Blue Feather's eyes fell on the empty moss where Hoogol had lain. She realized then that there was no going back to the way things had been—for her, for Ragtag, or for any of them.

A short distance away, Tattler was saying farewell to Headstrong. "The sparrows are yours to command. Lead them well."

"I will," Headstrong replied. "But just until you get back.

There's only one leader of the Winged Regiment, and that's you."

Tattler lowered her voice. "Keep an eye on Bobtail. Even though he's Blue Feather's son, I still think he's inexperienced and a bit too concerned with his own glory."

"Don't worry, I'll keep him in line," Headstrong replied. "You just keep your eye on that crow. No doubt he'd betray you and Ragtag at the first opportunity."

"A part of me hopes he does," Tattler said. "I'd like nothing better than to go one-on-one with him."

Loki hopped forward, realizing he was the subject of their discussion. "We're wasting time," he complained. "It's almost dawn!"

"We'll leave when Ragtag is ready," Tattler said. "And not a moment sooner. Do I make myself clear, crow?"

"My name is Loki, not crow."

"I couldn't care less what you call yourself." Tattler turned her back on him as Ragtag flew over. "All set?"

Ragtag nodded. "The sooner we leave, the sooner we get back."

The clan leaders gathered around and wished them luck. Even the swans, who usually kept to themselves, glided over and wished them well.

Ragtag took a deep breath. "Let's go."

They took to the air and followed Loki across the lake. Watching the birds beneath the bridge slowly grow smaller, Ragtag felt his stomach turn to lead. Would he ever see any of them again? What was he doing? Why had he let his mother talk him into being the leader of the Feathered

Alliance? He felt crushed by the responsibility. Was he making a mistake by putting their fate into the hands of the crow who had betrayed them?

Ragtag thought of Hoogol and how the owl's youthful pride had led to his father's death and the destruction of his woodland home. Was he now making a similar mistake? Perhaps it was better to turn around and convince the clan leaders to flee the city, rather than put all their hopes in an eagle they might never find.

The swallow shook his head. No matter what happened, the birds of the city wouldn't flee. Too many had already died defending their home. Ragtag thought of Hoogol and Proud Beak, the sparrows lost over the river, the countless lives ruined, the eggs stolen, the nests raided and destroyed.

Anger welled up inside him. He wouldn't let the others down. He would return with Baldur and save the city or die trying. Ragtag was so intent on his thoughts that he didn't realize Loki and Tattler had slowed ahead of him. Suddenly he rammed into Tattler's tail and the two birds dropped with a squawk into the grass below.

"You okay?" Tattler said.

"Yeah, sorry," Ragtag replied sheepishly. "I wasn't paying attention."

Loki circled back and landed next to them. "What are you doing? We don't have time for games!"

"Be quiet," Tattler ordered.

Loki hopped beneath a bush and scanned the sky. "I told you we should have left earlier," the crow said. Then he added, "I would get out of sight if I were you."

Ragtag glanced up. Dawn was breaking over the city. High above, they could just make out what looked like a falcon wheeling through the clouds. Ragtag and Tattler hopped back and joined Loki beneath the bush.

"Surt?" Ragtag asked fearfully.

"I'm not sure," Tattler said, squinting her eyes. "Not that it really matters. No doubt there's more than one peregrine falcon in the empire, and they're all deadly."

"We can't risk flying in the open during the day," Loki said. "I told you we should have left earlier."

"Stop your whining!" Tattler hissed.

"Both of you be quiet," Ragtag interrupted. "We need to figure out how we're going to get to the waterfront."

"I'll take us through the back streets," Tattler said. "If we stick close to the ground, we should be okay."

"You wouldn't make it more than a block." Loki laughed.

"We sparrows know how to avoid raptors!"

"You sparrows have done nothing except get yourselves killed since the empire invaded!"

"Thanks to you!" Tattler roared, and lunged at the crow. Loki jumped back just as Ragtag came between them.

"Stop this bickering, both of you!"

Tattler averted her eyes. "Sorry, Ragtag."

"If you want me to lead you to the eagle," Loki said to Ragtag with a hint of superiority, "we have to do it *my* way. I'm not about to let myself get killed because of this sparrow's ignorance."

Tattler was about to retort, but Ragtag motioned for her to keep quiet.

"Lead the way," Ragtag said to Loki.

"Follow me," the crow replied. "And this time, try to keep up."

Loki's attention turned to the cars zooming along the road next to them. A truck lumbered to a stop in front of a red light.

"Come on!" Loki called, and took wing. Ragtag and Tattler followed him as he glided across the street and landed beneath the truck.

"This is your plan?" Ragtag asked as he stared up at the vehicle's vibrating underbelly.

"Fly!" Loki cried as the truck lurched into gear. The three birds took to the air and flew along beneath it. As the truck came to another red light, the birds once again landed.

"Some plan!" Tattler muttered.

"We can move freely through the city this way," Loki told Ragtag, ignoring Tattler. "The raptors can keep watch all they like. They'll never spot us!"

The truck jolted forward and again the birds took flight, matching its speed. As Ragtag skimmed just inches above the asphalt, he had to admit that a part of him admired Loki's intelligence. Using human vehicles to shield themselves from the birds of prey would never have occurred to him.

The truck turned a corner, and Ragtag and Loki perfectly matched the maneuver. But behind them, Tattler was finding it difficult to maintain a steady altitude. There was only a small margin of safety between the ground and the truck's undercarriage. Ragtag and Loki had longer wingspans, which allowed them to fly more slowly and with greater control.

Unfortunately for Tattler, the sparrow's small body was designed for speed. She was constantly in danger of either slamming into the truck or plowing into the road.

The truck turned again, this time heading in the wrong direction.

"Quick!" Loki yelled, and banked hard to the left. Ragtag and Tattler squawked as they narrowly missed being run over by the truck's tires. The three birds cut across the road and aligned themselves under a massive eighteen-wheeler heading north.

"How much longer?" Tattler shouted.

"Don't tell me you're tiring already?" Loki laughed. "I thought you sparrows were great warriors."

"Loki, stop it!" Ragtag ordered.

The eighteen-wheeler slowed and came to a stop at another light, allowing the birds to drop to the pavement. Loki crossed over to one of the giant wheels and peeked out.

"We're almost there," he said. "We'll have to risk flying in the open the rest of the way."

Ragtag and Tattler followed the crow as he left the safety of the truck and flew past the New England Aquarium. They landed on one of the wharfs and quickly dropped down into the pilings. From there they could safely survey their surroundings.

Something doesn't feel right, Ragtag thought as he glanced around. It took him a few seconds to realize what was bothering him: the silence. Normally, on a morning like this, the sky would be filled with gulls, but today the skies were empty and not a single *"keew-keew"* could be heard.

"Look!" Ragtag cried. High above them, several hawks were circling the Custom House Tower, one of the tallest buildings lining the waterfront. Something seemed to pique their interest, and they quickly dropped from sight.

"Now's our chance," Loki said. The birds took flight and headed out over the water.

"I was hoping we could hitch a ride on a boat," Loki yelled back. "But we're out of luck. We'll have to wing it!"

"What if those hawks spot us?" asked Ragtag.

"Nothing much we can do about it now," Loki replied. "We've got to put as much distance as possible between us and the city."

Loki gained altitude and headed east toward the rising sun. The sky was cloudless and bright blue. Beneath them, the birds could see white-capped waves rolling past. They were silent as they flew farther out over the harbor, lost in their own thoughts.

Ragtag stole a glance behind him. The city was growing smaller in the distance. He remembered when Hoogol had banished him and he had flown out to a ship, intent on running away. It had been only a few days ago, yet it felt like a lifetime. Now here he was again, determined to leave the city. Would he ever see Copley Square again? He felt his stomach tighten as he realized he was now farther from his home than he had ever been in his life.

Hod

Predators and Prey

The mouse knew she was tempting fate by emerging so late from her burrow. She had already made the dangerous journey across Copley Square once, having discovered a stash of chestnuts earlier that morning. Hidden near the ground in the hollow of an old tree, they were no doubt the forgotten treasure-trove of some absent-minded squirrel.

The little creature hesitated, whiskers trembling as her eyes searched for predators. Glancing back at her warm and comfortable burrow, its entrance safely tucked away under a park bench, she wondered if perhaps it might be better to wait for the cover of night.

She quickly put such thoughts aside. If she had discovered the stash of chestnuts, some other animal might also find them. Perhaps a greedy rat or a worthless squirrel who would leave her with nothing. Wouldn't it be safer to gather a few more now, just to be on the safe side?

Thinking more with her stomach than with her head, she came to a quick decision. The mouse took a deep breath and bolted out from under the bench. It was the last mistake she would ever make.

Surt plunged from the sky and snatched the unlucky mouse off the ground. Beating his powerful wings, the peregrine falcon quickly gained altitude and returned to the attic of the Old South Church.

Hugin and Munin moved closer as he landed, drooling at the sight of the meat. Surt looked up and hissed, forcing the merlins to step back. They had always done the hunting for the emperor, but Surt had put a quick end to that tradition. "The day I can't hunt my own food," he had snarled at the sisters, "is the day I die."

Surt ripped the mouse apart and wolfed it down. He was in a bad mood. He had hoped the death of Hoogol would be the blow that shattered the last of the clans' resistance. But now rumors had reached him that the Feathered Alliance had a new leader. The birds of the city were rallying around a new symbol—the young swallow named Ragtag.

How dare a swallow stand against a falcon! Surt swore to himself that he would find and crush their new leader. He would teach the birds of the city that there were consequences to opposing him.

Gunlad alighted on the window. He waited until the emperor had finished his meal, then moved forward.

"We've rounded up a number of swallows, as you ordered," the red-tailed hawk said. "Unfortunately it would appear the vast majority have gone into hiding."

"They've been warned," Surt said. He had a good idea who had given the warning. "What about Loki?"

"We haven't found him yet."

"When you do, see that he's brought to me." Surt regretted not having killed the crow when he'd had the chance. Oh, well, he thought. It was a mistake easily corrected.

"As you wish," Gunlad replied.

"Where are the swallows?"

"In the water tower with Hod."

"Take me there," Surt ordered. "I'll question them myself."

The raptors had discovered an abandoned water tower atop a building that was being used as a nesting site by a flock of pigeons. The pigeons had been promptly routed and the tank converted to a new holding area. A rusted pipe was the only way in or out. Unlike the church attic, the water tower was escape-proof.

Surt landed and followed Gunlad inside. Hod was standing guard over ten swallows, who cowered in front of him. They were fledglings, rounded up by the raptors after they had been separated from their parents during the takeover of the city.

Hod caught sight of Surt and bowed stiffly. Surt ignored him and crossed over to the swallows. "Where's Ragtag?"

"We don't know," one of them squeaked.

"You're lying!" Surt snarled. "Where are the clan leaders? Where are they hiding?"

The young birds sobbed in terror, unable to respond.

Gunlad moved closer to Surt. "Perhaps if I made an example of one, the others would be more forthcoming."

Hod moved forward. "I doubt they know much. They're just fledglings."

"Why, Hod," Surt said sarcastically. "Do I detect a note of compassion in your voice? Perhaps you feel sympathy for these young birds?"

"I feel no sympathy for swallows!" Hod replied.

"Excellent. Gunlad, make your example."

Hod turned away as Gunlad's talons flashed. One of the swallows screamed and then fell silent. It was over in a matter of seconds.

"I will ask you once more," Surt calmly told the survivors. "Where is Ragtag? Where are the clan leaders hiding?"

The birds mumbled incomprehensibly and hid their heads beneath their wings.

"This is a waste of time," Surt said in disgust, and headed for the exit.

"What should I do with them?" asked Gunlad.

"Kill them," Surt replied. "Let it be a lesson to the miserable birds of this city. Put out the word that no swallow shall be left alive. This is how the falcon emperor repays Ragtag."

"With pleasure," Gunlad said before Surt departed. The hawk turned toward the fledglings just as one of his lieutenants entered the tank.

"Sir, our scouts have returned from their patrols. They're ready to deliver their report."

"Not now," Gunlad replied.

"They say it's important. They claim to know where the gulls are hiding."

Hod jumped forward and indicated the swallows. "I'll do it."

Gunlad nodded and left with the hawk. Hod watched from the entrance of the tank as they flew off, then faced the fledglings. He glanced at the body of the one Gunlad had struck down. The kestrel was proud to be a bird of prey and had no problems with a clean kill, but this was nothing but butchery.

Hod turned and caught a glimpse of himself in a pool of water. His once-beautiful plumage had been ruined by the scar Surt had left on him after the clan leaders had escaped. The new emperor had banished him from the church attic, giving him these menial tasks as punishment.

Hod loomed over the sobbing birds and suddenly made up his mind. He was tired of Surt and sick of the empire.

"Get out of here," he said to the fledglings.

The swallows stared at him in shock.

"I said, get out!" Hod roared, beating his wings. One by one, they fluttered through the pipe and took to the air. The last of them was bolder than the rest.

"Come with us!" the swallow chirped. "If you join the Feathered Alliance, I'm sure they'll hide you."

"Join you?" Hod laughed. "Don't be a fool. I spared your lives because I wish to pay back the falcon emperor for an injustice, not because I have any sympathy for you or your alliance. Now get out of here before I change my mind!"

The swallow quickly flew through the pipe and hurried to catch up with his companions. Hod followed them out and watched as they vanished over the rooftops. He knew that once Surt learned of his betrayal, he wouldn't have long to live. But he didn't care. They would have to find him first.

I'll find a new home, Hod thought. Perhaps a patch of woods far from here, unspoiled by humans, where I can once again be free. He knew the chances of finding such a place were slim, but it was better than bowing before Surt for the rest of his life.

Spreading his wings, Hod took flight and deserted the empire.

The sun beat down from overhead, forcing Ragtag and Tattler to squint. The two companions followed Loki as he continued to head east.

They had been island hopping for several hours now. Loki had allowed them short breaks to rest and find food, but the breaks hadn't been long enough for Ragtag's liking. After they had crossed the harbor, the crow had veered south, and they were now following the shoreline.

"Do you mind slowing down?" Ragtag called to Loki. "You have a much greater wingspan!"

Loki glided for a while, allowing the smaller birds to catch up.

"We have to hurry," Loki said. "We need to be farther away before we can rest."

"But we haven't seen a raptor for hours," Ragtag protested. "How far east does the empire spread?"

"No farther than the city, but Surt has sentries in the outlying areas. We can't risk being spotted."

"I can't go any farther," Ragtag declared as his wings began to cramp. He had never been airborne so long.

"It's too dangerous to rest here," Loki replied.

"Ragtag gave you an order," Tattler yelled. "So find us a place. Now!"

The tone of her voice warned Loki not to argue. He changed course and glided out of the sky, heading for a sleepy village near the shore. Ragtag and Tattler followed as Loki landed atop a hill overlooking a town. The swallow misjudged the speed of his approach and bounced several times before finally sliding to a stop upside down in the grass.

"You okay?" Tattler asked as she landed next to him.

"I'm done for," Ragtag moaned. "I'm going to sleep here and now."

Loki walked over, trying hard not to laugh. "This is the new leader of the Feathered Alliance?"

"Nobody asked you!" Tattler retorted.

"I was just—"

"I don't care! If I wanted the opinion of a filthy crow, I would ask for it. Now get out of my sight!"

"You've got a real chip on your shoulder, don't you?"

Tattler hopped right up to Loki's face. "You going to do something about it?"

Loki didn't back down. The crow drew himself up and loomed over the sparrow. Ragtag opened one eye and rolled to an upright position.

"Tattler, back off," Ragtag said.

"No, it's all right," Loki replied, without taking his eyes off Tattler. "I'm sure I can handle one *female* sparrow."

Tattler slammed into Loki so fast the crow didn't know what hit him. The two birds clawed at each other before Ragtag separated them.

"What is it with you and crows?" Loki demanded as he hopped back and nursed a bite mark on his wing.

"You actually dare ask me that?" Tattler cried. "You betrayed us all!"

"No, it's more than that," Loki said. "It's not just me. It's *all* crows. You're fueled by hatred."

"And proud of it!"

"Loki," Ragtag said. "Tattler has good reason to hate your clan."

"Why?"

"Because they orphaned her."

"Dirty filthy crows!" Tattler exploded before Ragtag could continue. "Crows like you killed my parents. Cowards! They outnumbered them three to one."

"I believe it's called survival of the fittest," Loki said.

"It had nothing to do with survival! The crows laughed and mocked my parents as they killed them. They weren't interested in food! I can still hear them cackling about how they hated sparrows, how they thought my clan overran the city with our numbers, and how it was their duty to reduce our population!"

"I wasn't involved."

"You're a crow! That's all that counts!" Tattler shouted, and flung herself at him again. Ragtag leaped forward, forcing them apart for a second time.

"Enough!" Ragtag yelled. "We need to work together if we're ever going to get back home. Fighting among ourselves is crazy!"

Tattler hopped away as Loki turned to Ragtag. "I can't

lead you to the eagle if she's going to sabotage me every step of the way!"

"I'll talk to her," Ragtag promised. "Why don't you see if you can find us some food? Maybe one of those houses has a feeder."

Loki muttered something about not being their servant as he flew off. Ragtag waited until he was gone, then joined Tattler. For a long moment, neither spoke.

"Tattler, I know how you feel," Ragtag began.

The sparrow whirled on him. "Do you? Somehow I doubt it! Your parents weren't slaughtered in front of your eyes. You don't wake up in the middle of the night with their screams echoing in your ears!"

Ragtag looked away.

"My entire life I've fought against the crows," Tattler continued. "When others played, I trained. Day after day, I pushed myself to the limit. I'm the youngest sparrow and the first female to ever win the command of the Winged Regiment, and I did it so that I could protect the alliance from the crows, not serve them!"

"The crows are no longer our enemy," Ragtag replied. "Surt is the one we have to fear now, not Loki."

"Loki's still treacherous!" Tattler retorted. "He may have fooled you into thinking he's on our side, but he'll never fool me."

With that, she took wing and flew a short distance away. Ragtag sighed and slumped over in the grass. If he couldn't get Tattler and Loki to cooperate, what hope was there of finding Baldur and getting back to the city before Bobtail launched his attack? He desperately wished Hoogol were still alive. The great horned owl had always seemed to know what to do.

Ragtag's thoughts were suddenly interrupted by Loki's return.

"Time to go!" the crow yelled.

"Loki," Ragtag said. "The only thing that could get me off this hill would be Surt himself."

"Well, it's not Surt, but it's pretty close."

Ragtag froze as he heard the scream of a raptor. A northern goshawk was circling high overhead.

Tattler flew back to them. "You fool!" she spat at Loki. "Ragtag told you to *find* breakfast, not turn us into it!"

"Oh, yes. I brought her here on purpose just to annoy you," Loki replied.

"Quiet, you two," Ragtag whispered. "Has she seen us?"

Just then, the goshawk folded her wings and plunged toward them.

"Does that answer your question?" Loki replied. The crow bolted for the woods, his companions on his tail. They zipped in and out of the branches and underbrush.

Behind them, the larger raptor had to slow herself in order to maneuver through the obstacle course. Even so, the goshawk was quickly closing the space between them. Ragtag glanced back in alarm. He didn't have Tattler's speed or Loki's strength.

"Loki, do something!" Ragtag yelled. "I can't outrun it."

A distant squeal drew the crow's attention. Sunlight flashed off something metallic moving through the trees.

Loki banked hard and broke from the cover of the woods.

Ragtag and Tattler emerged behind him and followed the crow as he made a beeline for the receding train. Loki reached the last car, landed, and flattened himself to avoid being blown off.

"Come on!" he yelled. Ragtag and Tattler strained their muscles to the breaking point. The two birds finally reached the train and collapsed next to each other. Behind them, the goshawk screamed in frustration as the train picked up speed. The raptor fell behind and finally vanished from sight.

"Keep your wings down; otherwise you'll be blown off," Loki said as the wind whistled over their heads.

Ragtag tried to keep himself as low as possible. He was exhausted. They had gone out of the frying pan straight into the fire, and now they were hitching a ride on a metallic monster that was traveling faster than he had ever flown in his life.

The swallow hunkered down and used Loki's larger bulk as a shield from the wind. Against his will, he found his eyes slipping closed. He soon fell into a restless sleep and dreamt he was being chased by hundreds of angry goshawks.

It was only when the train slowed that Ragtag opened his eyes. The sun was lower in the sky. Tattler shook herself awake next to him, looking embarrassed at also having fallen asleep.

Loki was already on his feet, the train's slower speed allowing him to stand. Ragtag and Tattler jumped up and looked around. They were pulling into a town nestled next to the ocean.

"Where are we?" Ragtag asked.

"End of the line!" Loki said. "Come on, it's only a short flight from here."

Ragtag and Tattler exchanged a look of joy and followed Loki as he took to the air. Soon they would find Baldur, and with any luck, they would all be back in the city with plenty of time to spare.

A gust of wind from the east brought with it the smell of the sea. The trees thinned and the houses were left behind. Ahead of them stretched a vast beach of pearly white sand. Far out at sea, a mass of dark clouds hovered over the horizon. Nothing else could be seen.

Ragtag and Tattler landed and joined Loki at the water's edge. "I don't understand," Ragtag said. "Where's Baldur?"

"I told you," Loki replied. "We have to cross the Great Water first."

"What do you mean?" Tattler cried.

"We've already crossed it," Ragtag added. "All those islands—"

"No, no, no!" Loki sighed and rolled his eyes. "I know this is difficult, but try to keep up. That was only the *harbor*. Baldur's being kept by the humans on the other side of the Great Water."

The crow pointed a wing at the seemingly endless ocean. "And *that* is the Great Water."

Bragi

Sacrifice

R ain fell in sheets and ragged clouds whipped over the city of Boston. Three red-tailed hawks braved the weather, flying in formation as they passed over the common. They were searching for any signs of the alliance. Since the escape of the clan leaders, the raptors had been on high alert. Rumors had reached the birds of prey that the clans had established a secret base right under their wings, but try as they might, they couldn't find it.

Thunder rumbled in the distance. The hawks muttered to themselves as the winds picked up and made flying difficult. No doubt their emperor was tucked away in the warmth and shelter of the church attic while they were out doing all the work.

The raptors passed over the stone bridge in the public garden, not suspecting what lay beneath. They caught sight of the swans gliding across the lake. The hawks didn't like the swans but were under orders not to bother them. Earlier a pair of harriers had attempted to chase the swans from the water and had been surprised when humans had come to their defense. The emperor didn't know what arrangement the swans had with the humans, but he preferred not to get involved.

The lead hawk urged his companions forward and the raptors beat their wings. As soon as the birds of prey were out of sight, the swans nodded in the direction of the bridge. Bobtail saw the signal and quickly joined Gini and Headstrong. The three of them crossed over to a tree where Bragi and a dozen pigeons stood waiting.

"I'll come right to the point," Bobtail said with an air of authority. "As you know, it's imperative that we—"

"What's 'imperative' mean?" one of the pigeons interrupted.

"It means absolutely necessary," Headstrong said.

"Yes, as I was saying," Bobtail continued. "It's imperative that we get the Winged Regiment back together. The sparrows are hiding in the towns and villages outside the city. We've dispatched robins, starlings, and swifts with secret messages, but none have returned."

The pigeons murmured uneasily, their heads bobbing up and down.

"I'm not going to lie to you," Bobtail said. "We think they were captured or worse. Which is why we need you."

"B-b-but," Bragi stammered, "we're just pigeons!"

"Exactly why you can succeed where they failed," Headstrong said.

The pigeons blinked.

"The emperor has restricted the movements of all the clans except the pigeons," Bobtail explained. "There are just too many of you. He also thinks you're too stupid to help the alliance."

Bragi's beak fell open.

"We know they're wrong," Gini said helpfully.

"Pigeons are the only birds who can travel freely throughout the city," Bobtail said. "That's why we need you for an important mission. You have to deliver a secret message to the sparrows."

"Important missions, secret messages," Bragi said as she shook her wings in frustration. "But we're just pigeons!"

"Cowardly pigeons!" her flock added.

Headstrong moved forward. "You're cowards only if you think you are. Look at Ragtag! He's risking his life right now to bring back an eagle."

"That's right," Bobtail said. "What happens if he returns and we're not ready?"

"We know you're scared," Headstrong continued. "We all are. I have eight cousins in the Winged Regiment. They can't stay hidden forever. It's only a matter of time until the Talon Empire finds them. We need to act now!"

"But . . . but . . ."

"Yes?"

"We're just—"

"Pigeons!" Bobtail yelled. He was beginning to lose his temper. "We already know that. So tell me, as pigeons, how long do you think it'll be before the raptors grow tired of the taste of mice?"

The pigeons whispered among themselves. Finally Bragi waddled forward. "What exactly do we have to do?"

Ragtag and Tattler followed Loki as he flew under the dark clouds. Lightning flashed across the sky, blinding in its intensity. It was followed a split second later by a crash of thunder.

The birds struggled to remain airborne as torrential rains drenched their feathers. Bolts of lightning provided glimpses of white-capped waves far beneath them.

At any other time, Ragtag would have been happy to ride the storm, but now he found himself peering through the wind and rain trying to keep track of his companions. Loki's jet-black feathers didn't help, and Tattler was so small she could barely be seen.

Ragtag fought to maintain his heading as the wind buffeted him. His companions had it easier. The crow had a greater wingspan, and the sparrow's speed meant she was in no danger of being outdistanced by the others.

"I can't see a thing," Ragtag shouted over the howling wind. "How much farther?"

"Hard to say," Loki yelled back. "I'm not even sure we're headed in the right direction."

Ragtag's spirits dropped. For all they knew, they were flying in circles.

"My wings are too wet!" Tattler gasped. "We have to land."

"Land?" Loki cackled. "Do you have a specific wave in mind, or should I pick one?"

"Whose stupid idea was this?" Tattler asked. "If I didn't know any better, I would think you were trying to get us killed!"

"Not everyone, just you!"

"I should never have gone along with this insane plan of yours. As if we could just fly across the Great Water!"

Loki's response was drowned out by a rumble of thunder. Ragtag didn't bother to come between the two. He was concentrating on just keeping up.

The swallow glanced beneath him. For a second, he thought he saw a light on the surface of the water. There it was again!

"Tattler, Loki!" Ragtag cried. "Look!"

The birds squinted to see through the driving rain. A light was winking somewhere below them.

"Do you see it?" Ragtag asked.

"Yes!" Tattler shouted back. "What is it?"

"Only one way to find out!"

Ragtag furled his wings and plunged through the clouds, Tattler and Loki behind him. As they flew closer, they could make out a small fishing boat tossing on the waves.

The boat rose on a wave's crest with stomach-churning speed and hung there for a few seconds. Then it dropped, vanishing into an inky trough, only to rise up once again.

The three exhausted birds headed for the boat. Ragtag knew landing would be dangerous. Gusts of wind were blowing them in every direction, and the ship was lurching precariously on the waves.

Tattler fluttered down first. As usual, she made a perfect landing. Ragtag tried to join her on the bridge, but the boat shifted at the last second. With a squawk, he fell into the sea.

"Ragtag!" Tattler yelled.

Before she could react, Loki swooped down. The crow grabbed hold of Ragtag with his claws, lifted him out of the water, and dropped him next to Tattler.

Loki flapped his wings desperately to maintain his position. But the howling winds pushed him sideways, and he was forced to land on the ship's prow.

"Ragtag, are you okay?" Tattler asked.

Ragtag coughed up water and sputtered, "Yes, thanks to Loki."

He couldn't believe it. Loki had saved his life. Ragtag glanced at the crow, then saw what was approaching behind him. "Loki, watch out!"

Loki whirled and raised his wings just as a huge wave crashed over the bow. When the water receded, the crow was gone.

"Loki!" Ragtag screamed. He and Tattler flew around the heaving ship, desperately searching for any sign of their companion. Loki had vanished.

"It's no use," Tattler shouted through the rain. "He's gone!"

Ragtag followed Tattler back to the boat. The two companions landed on the bridge, drenched and shivering in the cold. Another wave hit. Spray crashed over the bridge and the birds had to take to the air to avoid being washed overboard.

"We've got to find shelter," Tattler yelled over the howling wind. "We'll be washed out to sea if we stay here!"

"Look!" Ragtag shouted. An open window led inside. "We'll have to risk it!"

The birds fluttered through the window. A human stood

behind the ship's wheel. Ragtag and Tattler landed and peered up at him, wondering what he would do. When the giant man caught sight of them, he roared with laughter. Grabbing a bottle of water, he poured some into a dish and set it down.

"Ragtag, don't!" Tattler warned as the swallow drank deeply.

"It's okay," Ragtag said. "He's a friend."

"How do you know?" Tattler whispered when the man had turned back to the wheel.

"I just do," Ragtag said. He really didn't, but he was too exhausted and thirsty to care.

Tattler sipped some of the water while Ragtag's thoughts turned back to Loki. He couldn't believe the crow was gone. Loki had sacrificed his life to save him.

A flock of pigeons gathered in Copley Square, cooing nervously as thunder rumbled in the distance. High above them, hawks peered through the rain, keeping watch from the roof of the Boston Public Library.

The birds of prey had given up trying to control the movement of the pigeons. There were simply too many of them. Surt had ordered the hawks to keep an eye on them, but even this command had gone unheeded. It was obvious to the raptors that the pigeons were too dumb to plan anything by themselves.

Bragi wanted to prove them wrong. Other clans had made far greater sacrifices for the Feathered Alliance. Now it was the pigeons' turn. She moved through the crowd, whispering last-minute words of encouragement. Finally she flapped her wings. Her flock rose through the rain, circled the belfry of the Old South Church, and headed south.

The raptors watched them depart. One of Gunlad's lieutenants turned to him questioningly. "Sir?"

"Let them go." Gunlad yawned. "Stupid pigeons. If they want to venture out in this weather, good riddance."

As the pigeons left Copley Square, Bragi was relieved there was no sign of pursuit. "Remember the plan," she called. "And good luck!"

The pigeons scattered to the wind. Bragi headed away from Copley Square, leaving the city's skyscrapers behind. The storm lessened in intensity as she beat her wings and glided over the Charles River.

Beneath her the buildings thinned and the land turned green with patches of trees and grass. Bragi found a small town and landed near its common.

She tried to remember what Headstrong had told her. The Winged Regiment was divided into twelve brigades. When Tattler had given the order to disperse, each brigade had retreated to one of the towns lying outside the city. There they would stay in hiding, always keeping a sentry posted near the town's center to await messages.

Bragi took a deep breath and chirped the secret code Headstrong had taught her. There was no response. She chirped again, hoping she was pronouncing it properly.

"*Pssst!*" someone hissed. The pigeon whirled. One of Headstrong's many cousins hopped out of his hiding spot and quickly flew over.

"The Winged Regiment has been ordered to regroup and

return to the city under cover of night," Bragi said. "Meet at the lake with the bridge before the dawn of the next full moon. The swans will have further instructions."

"I'll pass along the message," the sparrow replied. "We'll be there."

The sparrow flew off, and Bragi started foraging for food, feeling very pleased with herself. Little did she know that hidden in a tree above her, a black-hawk had been watching her every move. The raptor dropped off the branch and swooped down.

"Nooooo!" Bragi screamed.

As the black-hawk climbed back into the sky, only a few feathers marked the spot where the pigeon had stood.

Egrets

A Means to an End

Ragtag awoke to find the human gone. Through the window, he saw that the boat was anchored in a small harbor. The sky was blue and the sun had already risen. The storm was over.

He jumped up, horrified he had slept so long. Tattler was dozing next to him. "Tattler, wake up!"

Tattler yawned and stretched her wings. "Where are we?"

"I don't know. You okay?"

"Yes, you?"

"I think so. . . ." Ragtag's voice trailed off. He glanced around, half expecting to see Loki's jet-black plumage and hear the crow's familiar cackle.

"Poor Loki," Ragtag said.

"Yeah," Tattler replied, then added, "Never thought I'd hear myself say that."

"Come on, we can't stay here."

Tattler followed Ragtag out the window, startling the human, who was throwing nets out into the water. He waved to the birds as they flew past and headed for the shore.

"Where are we?" Tattler asked.

"I don't know," Ragtag replied. "We'd better stop and get our bearings."

They landed on the beach and looked around. The landscape was alien to the city birds. Strange bushes dotted the shore, and there was nothing but towering sand dunes as far as the eye could see.

Ragtag had a sinking feeling. Since leaving the city, they had traveled farther than he'd ever thought possible, yet it seemed they were no closer to their destination.

"What now?" Tattler asked.

"What do you mean?"

"What do you mean, what do I mean? You're the leader!"

"So?"

"So lead!"

"How am I supposed to lead when I don't even know where we are?"

"I told you this was a fool's quest!" Tattler shouted. "We should never have left the city!"

"Nobody forced you to come," Ragtag replied. "It wasn't my idea for our guide to get washed overboard!"

"But it happened!" Tattler said. "So how do we deal with it? Ragtag, we're lost! We have no hope of finding your eagle. Not only that, we have no hope of getting home!"

"Don't tell me what I already know!" Ragtag said. He fluttered onto a piece of driftwood and scanned the shore.

Tattler alighted next to him. "Headstrong will have the

Winged Regiment regrouped by now. They're going to be slaughtered!"

"Be quiet and let me think!" Ragtag yelled. He didn't mean to sound so harsh, but he had reached his breaking point. The entire quest for the eagle had been a long shot to begin with. Now that Loki was gone, it seemed hopeless.

"What are you going to do?" asked Tattler as she hopped up and down in frustration.

"What am *I* going to do? You mean what are *we* going to do! Why do I always have to be the one who makes the decisions?"

Tattler's beak fell open in astonishment. "Because you agreed to be our leader, and I agreed to follow you. Headstrong was right. I should have taken command. You're nothing but a child!"

Ragtag angrily collided with the sparrow. The two birds fell off the wood, pecking at each other as they rolled across the sand. But their fight came to a sudden end when they bumped into a half-dozen egrets, who glared at them from atop their stiltlike legs.

"Well, well," one of the egrets said with a sneer. "What have we here?"

Ragtag and Tattler were speechless. The egrets were enormous, larger even than the raptors. Long drooping feathers adorned the lower part of their backs, and their necks curved strangely.

"Trespassers!" a second egret shouted.

"Let the blue heron deal with them," yelled a third.

"Yes, yes, to the blue heron we go," they all said.

Ragtag and Tattler tried to take flight, but the egrets lunged forward and grabbed them by the back of their necks. No matter how much Ragtag struggled, he couldn't break free. He finally gave up and watched his captors with fascination as he and Tattler were whisked away. The egrets had legs that bent backward, making them look as if they were walking in reverse.

Ragtag glanced over at Tattler. He could see that she, too, had given up trying to free herself and was waiting to see where they were being taken. He felt a pang of regret over their argument. They had allowed themselves to be caught off-guard in a foreign land.

"The fledglings are missing," Gunlad said as Surt stalked back and forth through the attic of the Old South Church.

"What about Hod?"

"He was seen flying south alone."

"Deserter!" the falcon snarled. "Spread word that if he's found, he's to be killed on sight."

"With pleasure, m'lord."

"In a way, I'm glad he's gone. That kestrel was weak. He didn't have the backbone to serve the empire." Surt stopped pacing and looked appraisingly at Gunlad. "Unlike you. Now that I've taken the throne, I suppose I shall have to designate an heir. I choose you, Gunlad. Serve me well, and one day a red-tailed hawk will rule the Talon Empire."

Gunlad bowed. "You honor me."

A black-hawk suddenly flew in and dumped a pigeon on the floor. Bragi was trembling with fear but otherwise unhurt.

"M'lord," the black-hawk said to Surt. "I caught this pigeon talking to a sparrow in one of the outlying towns. I believe it was passing along a message."

"Well done," Surt replied, and dismissed him with a wave. The black-hawk bowed and flew out.

Bragi looked around, terrified at being back in the attic, alone this time. Any thoughts of escape were crushed as Surt leaped forward and grabbed hold of her.

"P-please d-don't eat m-me!" Bragi begged.

The raptors in the attic howled with laughter. Surt brought his hooked beak closer to the pigeon's head. "If you don't want to be consumed . . . you'd better start talking."

"I'll te–tell you everything—"

"What did you say to that sparrow?"

"Nothing. I was just—"

As Surt squeezed his talons, Bragi cried, "We're c-c-carrying m-messages for the F-f-feathered—"

"Go on!" Surt demanded. "What type of messages?"

"S-s-secret messages f-for the Winged Regiment t-to regroup on the morning after the f-f-full . . . f-f-full . . ."

Surt shook the pigeon mercilessly. "Spit it out! I don't have all day."

". . . full moon for a surprise attack," Bragi sobbed. She knew she was betraying the alliance, but she couldn't help herself. Pigeons were horrible at keeping secrets even at the best of times, and having a peregrine falcon shaking her certainly didn't help.

Bragi squeezed her eyes shut and waited for the final blow. It never came. Surt turned his back on the quivering bundle and motioned for Gunlad to join him out of earshot.

"The fools," Surt whispered. "We beat them once over the river. Do they really think they can defeat us in a second battle?"

"Give me a few minutes alone with this pigeon," Gunlad proposed, "and I promise you the location of their secret headquarters."

"No," Surt replied. "We would take their leaders, but the sparrows would still be at large." The falcon looked thoughtfully at Bragi. "I have an idea. We're going to let this flying rodent escape. . . ."

Ragtag and Tattler were whisked over a dune. Ahead of them lay a shipwrecked boat, half buried in the sand. The egrets bent their long necks and carried their captives in through an opening in the wood. The interior had long since rotted away, leaving only a bleached hull that kept out the wind. A clear blue sky could be seen above them, and the prisoners wondered if they would get a chance to make a break for it.

Thoughts of escape dimmed as they were roughly dropped into a crowd of birds even stranger-looking than the egrets. Wrens, loons, and sandpipers all pushed forward to have a look at the newcomers.

"You okay, Ragtag?" Tattler asked.

"Yeah, you?"

"Yeah. Sorry about our argument."

"Me, too. What do you think they want?"

"No idea."

"Be quiet!" one of the egrets roared. "The blue heron will deal with you soon enough."

Ragtag and Tattler stared with a mixture of curiosity and fear at the foreign-looking birds. They didn't have to wait long for the arrival of the blue heron. A hush fell over the crowd, and the birds parted to reveal the oddest creature Ragtag had ever seen.

The blue heron dwarfed her subjects. Her plumage was blue-gray, except around her neck, which was tinged red. A giant white crest rose high above her head, giving her a dignified and regal look, and she had the same piercing eyes and swordlike beak as the egrets.

A wren quickly hopped forward and whispered in her ear.

"You were found trespassing upon my land," the heron said to Ragtag and Tattler. "Who are you? Why are you here?"

"I'm sorry," said Ragtag. "We didn't know this was your land."

The crowd broke into snickers. The blue heron wasn't amused. "Didn't know? Do you take me for a fool? Are you spies for those infernal crows?"

"We're not spies for anyone," Tattler said. "We were blown off course by a storm. We're lost."

Ragtag hopped forward. "My name's Ragtag. I'm the leader of the Feathered Alliance, a coalition of birds who live in the city across the Great Water."

The blue heron leaned forward with interest. "Did you say the Feathered Alliance?"

"You know of it?" Ragtag asked. If the shore birds knew of the Feathered Alliance, perhaps they would help.

"Of course I know of it!" the heron snapped. "Just because we live far from the city doesn't mean we're ignorant of its existence." She leaned so close that Ragtag could smell the fish on her breath. "But you're a liar. An old owl named Hoogol leads the Feathered Alliance."

"Hoogol is dead," Tattler said.

The crowd erupted at the news, forcing the blue heron to shout for silence. "Dead?" she repeated. "How?"

"He was killed by an empire of raptors," Ragtag said. "I was elected to take his place."

"Really? There must have been a shortage of qualified candidates. So tell me, little Ragtag, why are you so far from the city? Are you being pursued?" Her eyes narrowed. "Have you brought these predators to my shore?"

"No," Ragtag replied. "We're on a mission to find an eagle. His name is Baldur. I'm going to bring him back to the city to fight the birds of prey!"

The blue heron laughed and visibly relaxed. "A lone eagle won't prove much worth against the likes of the Talon Empire. Yes, you don't have to look so surprised. News of their advance has preceded you. This emperor . . ."

"Surt," Ragtag said.

"It seems to me," the blue heron said thoughtfully, "that this Surt would make a powerful ally if properly approached. Perhaps if he were given a gift. Say . . . the leader of the Feathered Alliance?"

"You wouldn't dare!" Tattler yelled, and hopped forward. A pair of egrets forced her back.

"Oh, I assure you I would," the heron replied.

"Coward!" Tattler shouted as she struggled against the egrets.

The blue heron ignored her and kept her eyes on Ragtag. "I'm sorry, young swallow. Try to understand, it's nothing personal. I simply must protect my own kingdom by whatever means I can. And you, I'm afraid, are one of those means."

"You think you can make a deal with Surt?" Ragtag asked quietly. "You wouldn't be the first. The Talon Empire is not interested in sharing power, only in taking it."

The blue heron paused to consider this. Ragtag detected an opening and hopped forward. "Join us! Help me find my eagle and we'll fight Surt together!"

The crowd watched their leader to see what she would do. The blue heron stared at Ragtag for a long time. Finally she said, "You remind me so much of myself at your age. I can still remember a time when I was as young and full of ideals as you are now. Luckily I outgrew them. I'm sorry, Ragtag, but ideals will only get you so far in life. Then they'll get you killed. Hoogol would be a good example, I think.

"Take a message across the Great Water," she ordered a sandpiper. "Inform the Talon Empire that we have a swallow named Ragtag in our custody. Tell Surt that the blue heron will personally hand him over as a token of respect and friendship between our two kingdoms."

"No!" Tattler screamed as the sandpiper hopped out.

"You have no idea what you've just done," Ragtag said.

"I have every idea," the heron replied, then turned to her egrets. "Keep them here until the raptors arrive."

The heron was about to depart when a sandpiper shouted a warning. Ragtag and Tattler glanced up, their spirits soaring as Loki plummeted out of the sky along with a murder of crows.

"Don't just stand there! Fly!" Loki yelled to his stunned companions while the crows dive-bombed the crowd, scratching wildly at the blue heron. With the crows distracting the shore birds, Ragtag and Tattler spread their wings and followed Loki up out of the boat and over the sands.

They skimmed between the dunes, zigzagging wildly to avoid pursuit. Finally, after putting some distance between themselves and the egrets, Loki glided to the ground and waited for Ragtag and Tattler to catch up.

"We thought you were dead!" Ragtag gasped, struggling to catch his breath.

"For a while, so did I," Loki replied. "I swallowed quite a bit of water and nearly drowned. When I resurfaced, the boat had vanished. So I kept on flying, and arrived just in time to watch you two getting into trouble again. Sorry for the delay, but it took me some time to find help."

"But how?" Ragtag asked, still not believing his eyes.

"I told you we crows stick together," Loki said. "I found them south of the harbor. It didn't take much coaxing to get them to help. They hate the blue heron. She's a big bully in these parts."

"She would have given us to Surt just to save her own miserable neck," Ragtag said.

"And Surt would have killed her without a second thought," Tattler added.

"Yes, well," Loki replied a bit uncomfortably. "We all make mistakes. Don't judge her too harshly. She thinks she's far more powerful and important than she really is. Now hurry! If you still want to find this eagle of yours, it's only a short distance to where the humans are keeping him!"

Bragi flew through the streets of Boston as fast as she could. In her excitement, she almost forgot what Headstrong had taught her. She quickly landed in a plaza crowded with pigeons. The instant the others saw her, they came together to form one giant mass of wings and feathers. Then, a few seconds later, they took to the air and scattered.

Bragi continued, confident that not even a hawk's keen eyes could have kept track of her. She banked sharply and entered the Public Garden. Instead of making a beeline for the bridge, however, she landed at the water's edge.

The two swans glided across the lake, seemingly ignoring her presence. When they reached the far end, one turned and nodded. Bragi quickly flew forward, confident that no raptors were watching.

Beneath the bridge, Bobtail was busy making plans with Headstrong and Gini. The other clan leaders gathered around Bragi as soon as she fluttered into the shelter. The pigeon was so agitated, she could barely talk.

"Calm down and take a deep breath," Bobtail said. "I can't understand a word you're saying."

The pigeon's head bobbed up and down even though she tried to calm herself. Finally she managed to blurt out, "I was captured and taken to the attic of the Old South Church!"

The birds froze in alarm.

"Don't worry," Bragi said. "I didn't lead them here. I'm not stupid, you know."

"Let me get this straight," Bobtail replied. "You were captured and brought before Surt?"

"That's right!" Bragi insisted. "The falcon emperor himself!"

The clan leaders crowded around her. Bragi suddenly found herself the center of attention, and she loved it. This must be what it feels like to be an important bird, she thought.

"What did you tell him?" Gini cried.

"Nothing, of course," said Bragi indignantly. "Oh, he tried to pry all sorts of secrets from me, but I wouldn't tell him anything. I kept my beak shut. I was very brave!" And in her own mind, she had been. An unfortunate fact about pigeons is that they tend to remember events the way they want to, not the way they really happened.

"How did you escape?" Bobtail asked.

"When Surt was done questioning me—mind you, I didn't tell him anything—I was pushed into a corner and held captive by two merlins. They were ferocious, vile creatures with cruel-looking beaks and the sharpest talons you can imagine!"

The pigeons around Bragi cooed appreciatively.

"Yes, we know," Bobtail said. "Just leave out the embellishments and get on with it."

"Embellishments? *Hmmph!*" Bragi snorted, then quickly continued, "After several hours, they fell asleep. Slowly, so I wouldn't wake them, I crept toward the window. It was very scary. One creak of those floorboards and that would have been the end of poor old Bragi."

"Poor old Bragi!" the pigeons chortled.

Bobtail and Headstrong were both tapping their feet impatiently, but Bragi would not be rushed. This was her moment in the spotlight, and she was determined to make it last as long as possible.

"Were you scared?" Blackcap chirped from a crowd of chickadees.

"Terrified!" Bragi said. "But I knew I had to be brave. I had to escape, because I had learned something very important, something that could save the Feathered Alliance!"

"What? What?" the pigeons asked with bated breath.

"Yes, what?" Bobtail asked. "Please tell us before we die of old age."

"While the falcon emperor was talking to those nasty raptors," Bragi said, ignoring Bobtail's quip, "I overheard him say that he was going to be hunting alone at the field with the obelisk tomorrow at dawn."

Bobtail exchanged a glance with Headstrong.

"One of the bigger and uglier hawks asked Surt if he wanted a guard," Bragi continued. "And do you know what the emperor did? He laughed! He said why would he need one? No bird in the city would have the courage to attack him!"

"You did well," Bobtail said, and Bragi beamed with pride.

"I'd say. We pigeons are braver than I thought."

She walked away and was instantly mobbed by her flock, who demanded she retell her story from the beginning. Bobtail watched as they vanished out the far side of the bridge.

"What do you think?" he asked Headstrong.

Headstrong snorted. "Hugin and Munin falling asleep and allowing a pigeon to escape? Not very likely."

"But what if it's true?" Gini chirped. "After all, they think pigeons are stupid. It's possible they might have let down their guard. And that information she overheard—"

"About Surt hunting at dawn?"

"If the falcon emperor is going to be alone and unguarded," Gini said, "is that an opportunity we can afford to pass up?"

"I think it's a trap," said Headstrong.

"It could be," Bobtail replied. "But I think Gini's right. We have to take the chance."

Headstrong shook his head. "Ragtag left you in command, Bobtail, but I strongly advise against this. Tonight the moon will be full. We should stick to the original plan and wait for your brother. He's due back at noon tomorrow."

"You're right about one thing," Bobtail said with a hint of annoyance. "Ragtag did leave me in command. And as commander, I say this is too good a chance to pass up! Send word to prepare for the attack. I want the Winged Regiment regrouped and in place at that field by *dawn*."

Headstrong was about to protest when Bobtail whirled on him. "That's an order!"

The sparrow's beak snapped shut, and he flew off. Bobtail and Gini watched as he vanished into the trees on the far side of the Common.

"He doesn't trust you," Gini said. "His loyalty lies with Ragtag and Tattler."

"It doesn't matter. As he said, Ragtag left me in command. Headstrong will do what needs to be done. And so will we! Wouldn't it be ironic if Ragtag were to return tomorrow at noon to find the war already won?"

"The Feathered Alliance would probably elect you their new leader."

Bobtail stretched his wings. "Yes," he said thoughtfully. "Yes, indeed."

Blue Heron

The Broken Promise

Ragtag and Tattler followed Loki across acres of woodlands, wetlands, and grasslands teeming with life. Every hill they passed seemed to deliver something new to marvel at.

What a beautiful place, Ragtag thought as he swooped left and right to capture insects in his beak. If it weren't for the blue heron and her egrets, this might be an ideal refuge for the Feathered Alliance.

Ragtag suddenly remembered Hoogol, and how the Talon Empire had conquered the woods of his youth, forcing him to flee to the city. And how now, many years later, the raptors were expanding their domain, sweeping over the city like a great tide.

These poor creatures, Ragtag thought as he spotted a flock of geese high overhead. They don't know the danger lurking just over the horizon. There could be no refuge here. If the Talon Empire is allowed to hold the city, it will be only a matter of time until they spread east.

"How much farther?" Ragtag yelled over the wind.

"Almost there," Loki shouted back.

They crossed a dune peppered with oddly shaped plants, then followed a road north until it finally ended in front of a domed building. Two cars and a van were parked out front.

Loki landed atop the roof. Ragtag and Tattler quickly joined him, and together the three gazed through a skylight. Six empty cages sat on a workbench in a large white room beneath them. A familiar-looking eagle was asleep in a seventh.

"Baldur!" Ragtag called, flapping his wings to try to get the eagle's attention. There was no sign of movement.

"Baldur!" Ragtag yelled again.

"Maybe he's dead," Loki said.

"He's asleep," Tattler replied. "Look, you can see him breathing."

Ragtag banged his beak against the glass in an attempt to wake Baldur. "I have to get in there."

Loki and Tattler combined their strength and used their beaks to raise the skylight. It slowly rose an inch.

"Higher!" Ragtag said as the birds redoubled their efforts.

"Hurry," Tattler grunted. "We can't hold it for long."

Ragtag flattened himself and slipped through. He dropped down and landed next to a table, his eyes blinking in the bright light. Strange instruments were strewn about, and the hum of machinery filled the air. There was no sign of humans.

Quickly he flew over to Baldur's cage. The last time Ragtag had seen him, the eagle had been injured and bleeding.

Now he was clean, his feathers groomed and his wounds healed. Ragtag was amazed anew at how large he was. He would be more than a match for Surt!

"Baldur," Ragtag said. The great bird rolled over and sighed. "Baldur!" Ragtag said louder. "Wake up!"

The only response was a loud snore. Ragtag glanced around the room. There was still no sign of humans. He didn't want to think what they would do to him if they found him here. A vision of himself trapped in a cage for the rest of his life sprang to mind.

"Baldur!" Ragtag cried. He grabbed the bars of the cage with his claws and fluttered his wings, shaking them as hard as he could.

The eagle came awake with a start. He sat up, yawned, then climbed onto his perch.

"Baldur!" Ragtag said.

Baldur looked around, trying to locate the source of the sound.

"Down here," Ragtag said, hopping about to get the eagle's attention. The eagle peered at the bird near his feet.

"Who are you?" Baldur asked sleepily.

"It's me, Ragtag!"

"Rag who?"

"Ragtag! Remember? I helped free you when you were trapped in the city!"

The eagle lowered his massive white head and peered at the swallow with curiosity.

"Well, I'll be!" Baldur declared. "It is little Ragtag."

Ragtag suddenly felt hurt. He remembered how Baldur

had promised to stay in the attic while he went to fetch the clan leaders and how he'd arrived with them to find the eagle gone. Everything that had happened since then—the invasion of the city, the death of Hoogol, their quest across the Great Water—could have been avoided. Even though he already knew the answer to his question, he had to hear it from the eagle himself.

"Where did you go?" Ragtag cried. "You promised me you would stay. I came back and you were gone. I trusted you!"

"I'm sorry, little Ragtag, but it wasn't my fault. The humans came as soon as you left. They brought me back here."

Baldur yawned again and stretched his wings. "Speaking of which, what are you doing here? You're a long way from the city. Are you on holiday? The beaches here are very nice, you know."

"I've come to find you!"

"Me?" the eagle said. "Why, I'm touched, of course. But whatever for?"

"We need your help," Ragtag told him. "The Feathered Alliance has been attacked by the Talon Empire. The city has been overrun. You've got to come back with me. You're our only hope!"

Baldur cocked his head to one side and gazed at the swallow. "I'd love to help you, Ragtag, I really would, but I'm afraid it's impossible at the moment."

"What? Why?"

"Something has happened since I was recaptured." The eagle indicated the cages next to him. "I'm no longer alone. I have a mate now. Her name is Freya, and I've been invited into her clan. I'm actually quite happy."

Ragtag stared at the empty cages.

"Oh, they're not here now," Baldur said in answer to his unasked question. "They've been released on an island south of here. I'm going to be joining them in a few days. So you see, I can't come with you. If the humans caught me trying to escape a second time, I might never get to see my beloved Freya again."

Ragtag glanced at the metallic object attached to Baldur's leg. "But you'll still have that thing attached to you," Ragtag said, indicating the device. "Don't you want to be free?"

"Well, yes, I guess you have a point. But to tell you the truth, I don't really care about being free any longer."

Ragtag was too stunned to reply.

"Being free and alone is quite depressing," the eagle continued. "I just can't bear the thought of being separated from Freya. She's very beautiful. I think you would like her. Maybe you'll meet her someday."

Ragtag fluttered his wings in anger. "You promised you'd help me!" he cried. "You gave me your word of honor you'd come to my aid if I ever asked!"

"And I would help, if it were in my power. But I just can't risk it. I'm awfully sorry about this problem you're having with these raptors. Maybe you can find another eagle who can help you?"

Ragtag's beak fell open. Find another eagle? He didn't know what to say. Baldur wasn't even listening. Ragtag had worried so much that he, Tattler, and Loki wouldn't be able to find him. The possibility that Baldur would refuse to return with them had never crossed his mind.

A key suddenly jiggled in the door to the lab.

"Thanks for visiting," Baldur said hurriedly. "If you're ever in the neighborhood again, do drop by and say hello."

Ragtag quickly darted behind some boxes as the door opened. A woman wearing a white coat entered, opened Baldur's cage, and removed him. Ragtag watched as the giant bird was fed and groomed. He waited until the woman's back was turned, then fluttered his wings to get the eagle's attention.

"Go away!" Baldur said. The sound attracted the woman, who cooed at the eagle, then placed him back in his cage.

Ragtag watched in despair as the cage was put on a cart and wheeled out of the room. The woman turned off the lights and shut the door, leaving the swallow alone in the dark. He shook himself out of his stupor and flew back up to the skylight. Tattler and Loki again used their beaks to raise the glass and Ragtag slipped out.

"Well?" Tattler asked breathlessly.

Ragtag stared at her. He didn't know what to say. How could he tell her that after all they had gone through, all they had sacrificed—the eagle had simply deserted them. The Feathered Alliance was doomed, and it was all his fault.

"He's not coming!" Ragtag finally managed to choke out.

"Why not?" Tattler asked.

Quickly Ragtag recounted what Baldur had told him.

"But that's not fair!" Tattler said. "He promised."

"I know," Ragtag said. "He said he wouldn't leave without Freya."

Loki yawned and stretched his wings. "Well, you gave it your best shot. Nobody can say you didn't try. Personally, I think the best thing for both of you to do is forget about returning to the city. This looks like a nice place to live. I think I'll—"

"Shut up, Loki!" Ragtag yelled. He suddenly felt a burning hatred for the crow. How could he even suggest they forget about the city? Bobtail and Blue Feather were there, risking their lives along with the rest of the clan leaders.

"Sorry," Loki mumbled.

"Loki, you kept your promise," Tattler said coldly. "You brought us to the eagle, and we thank you for that. You're free now."

"Free?" Loki repeated.

"Yes. We have no further need of you. Go your own way, and we'll go ours."

Tattler turned her back on the crow and tried her best to comfort Ragtag. Loki leaned on one foot, then the next, not quite knowing what to do.

A door slammed somewhere beneath them. The birds hopped to the edge of the roof and looked down. A man was loading Baldur's cage into the back of the van. As soon as the eagle was secure, he jumped into the driver's seat and started up the engine.

"What do we do now?" Tattler asked.

Ragtag wasn't ready to give up yet. "Follow that eagle!"

Ragtag and Tattler launched themselves from the roof as the van pulled out and headed down the road. Loki, not knowing what else to do, followed them at a distance.

The van picked up speed and headed away from the building. In front of them lay a deserted stretch of road. If they were going to do something, it would have to be now.

"Tattler, we have to stop Baldur at whatever cost!" Ragtag cried.

"Leave it to me!"

Tattler folded her wings and dove toward the road. At the last minute, she pulled up and flew straight through the van's open window, fluttering her wings in the driver's face.

Ragtag and Loki watched from above as the van started weaving erratically. It left the road, climbed a dune, and flipped onto its side. The back door fell open and Baldur's cage rolled out. The eagle protested loudly as his cage bounced down the road, finally coming to a stop upside down in the sand.

Ragtag spotted Loki trailing behind him. "Loki, can you work a lock?"

"*Hmmph,*" the crow replied. "I thought you didn't need me anymore?"

"Loki, please!"

"All right, all right. Although it has to be said, to suggest a crow can't work a lock is a bit of an insult."

Loki flew down to the cage and pecked at the handle while Ragtag watched the overturned van. He sighed in relief when he saw Tattler suddenly emerge from the window, followed by the unhurt driver.

"Tattler, you okay?"

"Don't worry about me!" the sparrow yelled as she continued to distract the driver.

Loki finally managed to get the cage open. Baldur sprang out, took flight, and landed atop a nearby telephone pole. Ragtag alighted next to him.

"How dare you!" Baldur shouted. "I have a good mind to rip you to shreds!"

"Baldur, please!" Ragtag said. "I had to do it. You've got to listen to me. If you don't return with us, hundreds of innocent birds are going to die! You gave me your solemn promise. You told me the promise of a bald eagle was the most sacred promise in the world!"

"It is, but I also promised Freya I would join her!" Baldur said. "I can't break my promise to her to fulfill the one I made to you. I'm sorry, Ragtag, I really am, but I won't leave her behind."

And with that, Baldur took off and headed south at a speed Ragtag could never hope to match. Tattler fluttered up and landed next to him. The two birds watched as the eagle vanished into the clouds.

"What happened?" Tattler asked.

"He's not coming," Ragtag replied.

"Then we've failed! It's over, Ragtag. We've lost."

Loki landed next to them. "I hate to tell you this, but we're also out of time."

The birds gazed with a sinking heart at the full moon.

Ragtag, Tattler, and Loki flew north, following the coast to a small village nestled at the water's edge. There they found an outbound ferry on its way back to the city.

The three birds landed on the bridge of the ship. None of them spoke for a long time. Ragtag watched as Loki flapped down to the bow and spread his wings to feel the spray coming off the waves. The swallow felt embarrassed about his earlier outburst and had apologized to the crow. Loki had stuck with them after Baldur had flown off. He had told them that it was only because he, too, wanted to return to the city. Ragtag had the strange feeling that the crow was sad at the prospect of their separation.

Whatever the reason, Ragtag thought, he was glad Loki was still with them. Loki had made inquiries among the local crows. Without their help, they would never have been able to locate the right ferry to return them to the city.

The swallow glanced up at the moon hanging in the sky. Even if the ferry traveled at top speed, he doubted that they would get back in time to prevent the Winged Regiment's attack. Bobtail, Headstrong, and the sparrows would all be killed.

I've failed, Ragtag thought. He remembered his mother's words about how he was a symbol of hope—the young swallow who would defeat the Talon Empire. For a while, Ragtag had almost believed in his own myth. Now his wings sagged in despair. Bobtail and the clan leaders would launch their attack at noon, expecting Ragtag to arrive with his eagle.

But there would be no eagle. Baldur was gone. Even if the eagle did change his mind, there was no way he could reach the city in time. The Winged Regiment would be crushed and the clan leaders killed. The Feathered Alliance had come to an end.

Ragtag thought of Hoogol, of the great weight that the old owl had carried for so many years. Hoogol's father had died thinking he had been betrayed by his son. And now Blue Feather, Bobtail, and the others would die thinking Ragtag had failed them. And they would be right.

For the first time in his life, Ragtag realized what a horrible burden it was to be a leader. He had always envied Hoogol for the power he wielded and for the respect and admiration he commanded. Now he realized the price of power.

"You did your best, Ragtag," Tattler said. "It's not your fault."

"It is my fault," Ragtag replied quietly. "For better or for worse, I accepted the leadership of the Feathered Alliance. I told the clans I would bring back an eagle. I thought I had worked everything out. I thought I could be just like Hoogol. What a fool I am. I'm nothing but a pathetic swallow."

Tattler shook her head and sighed. "I can't believe Baldur just flew off."

Ragtag's gaze fell on Loki, standing proudly on the bow of the ship as it rose and fell with the waves. Hoogol had been right about him.

"Loki risked his life twice to save me, while Baldur broke his promise," Ragtag muttered. "What sort of a world is it when a crow proves more honorable than an eagle?"

The Trap Is Sprung

One of Headstrong's relatives hopped out from beneath a Dumpster and cautiously scanned her surroundings. Satisfied that there were no predators in sight, she chirped to her comrades. Ten more sparrows appeared and took off, hugging the ground as they made their way through Boston. The sun hadn't yet risen and the streets were still deserted. The sparrows headed north, crossed the Charlestown Bridge, and entered Bunker Hill.

Headstrong was waiting for them. He greeted his relatives and the others warmly, then quickly directed them to join the sparrows who were already camped out in the trees surrounding the park. He watched with pride as they disappeared into the foliage.

The Winged Regiment had been secretly slipping back into the city for the past two days. Traveling in groups of ten or fewer to minimize casualties in case they were intercepted, all twelve brigades had been able to reenter without being detected.

Headstrong stared at the dark obelisk towering over the park. The stone pyramid had a square base and sides that came together in a point high above. He wondered why the humans would build such an object. It served no purpose, as far as he could tell.

A flutter of movement pulled him away from his thoughts. Bobtail and Gini flew over the open field and landed next to him.

"Are you trying to give us away?" Headstrong said, unable to keep the annoyance from his voice. "Our presence here is supposed to be a secret, and you're flying around in the open!"

"You worry too much," Bobtail told him, and yawned. "Besides, nobody's here."

"That's right," Gini added. "Bobtail knows what he's doing."

Headstrong glared at the starling but said nothing. Soon after Ragtag had left, Bobtail had declared Gini to be his second-in-command. Headstrong disliked the way she was always following Bobtail around. It reminded him of the way Bobtail used to fawn over Proud Beak.

Headstrong had protested Gini's promotion, but Bobtail had overruled him. "I'm in command now," he'd said.

Headstrong had wanted to retort, "Only until Ragtag returns," but had kept quiet. He remembered what Tattler had told him: it was his job to keep an eye on Bobtail.

"Relax, Headstrong," Bobtail said when he realized the sparrow was fixated on him. "So far everything's gone smoothly."

"That's right," Gini added. "Bobtail's plan has been a great success."

"A great success?"

"Absolutely," Bobtail replied, ignoring the sarcasm in the sparrow's voice. "Thanks to my careful planning, we were able to regroup the Winged Regiment without losing a single bird."

"Don't you think that's a bit odd?"

"What do you mean?"

"I mean, this has all been too easy. As for our success, Surt hasn't even arrived yet. What if he doesn't show up?"

"Stop being so negative," Bobtail replied. "Surt will be here. And with a bit of luck, we'll catch him completely off-guard."

The morning sun appeared over the trees, and the birds took cover. Bobtail felt optimistic as he looked at the sparrows hidden around him. Leading the Feathered Alliance came naturally to him. He believed it was obvious to everyone that he was the real successor to Hoogol, not Ragtag. His plans were perfect in his mind, and he refused to even consider that something might go wrong.

His thoughts were suddenly interrupted by Gini's shout. All eyes turned to the field. A ripple of excitement passed through the sparrows. Surt had appeared and was slowly walking through the grass, alone and unguarded.

"Everyone get ready," Bobtail whispered.

Word was quickly passed through the ranks, and the sparrows tensed.

"Wait for my command," Bobtail said as some of the more eager sparrows spread their wings.

They all watched Surt peck at the grass.

"I don't like this," Headstrong muttered. "A falcon always hunts from the air. Why is he on the ground?"

"He's overconfident," Bobtail whispered. "He doesn't think anyone would have the courage to attack him. He's about to get the surprise of his life!"

Surt continued to move deeper into the park, seemingly unaware of the danger around him.

"Now!" Bobtail yelled.

"All sparrows!" Headstrong barked. "Attack! Attack!"

More than a hundred sparrows launched themselves from the trees and zoomed toward the falcon emperor. Surt laughed as he saw them approach. He spread his wings but made no move to flee.

A hundred yards separated the sparrows from the falcon. Then fifty. Then only twenty! Surt suddenly threw back his head and screamed at the top of his lungs. *"Keeek-kek-kek!"*

Forty birds of prey launched themselves from their hiding spots atop the buildings opposite the park. Screeching furiously, they beat their wings and hurtled toward the Winged Regiment. The two armies collided in midair, the panicked chirps of the sparrows drowned out by the triumphant screams of the raptors.

"It's a trap!" Headstrong shouted as he dodged a hawk's talons. The sparrows darted about in confusion as the birds of prey swooped through them.

"We've been tricked!" Gini cried, suddenly finding herself face-to-face with Gunlad. This wasn't what she'd had in mind when Bobtail had asked her to be his second-in-command. The starling shrieked and bolted away.

"Gini, where are you going?" Bobtail yelled. She didn't answer, and Bobtail soon found himself occupied with a sharpie. He managed to escape, but a pair of sparrows behind him weren't as fortunate.

Bobtail stared in shock as their bloodied feathers floated to the ground. Surt glided overhead, laughing as the sparrows were decimated.

"Bobtail, what do we do?" a sparrow cried. "Bobtail?"

Bobtail didn't answer. He hovered in midair, the screams and cries of the dying birds echoing around him.

"Bobtail, snap out of it!" Headstrong yelled as he flew up beside him.

Bobtail turned to him with a dazed look on his face. "Signal the retreat! Order the sparrows to scatter."

"No! We'll never be able to rally them again. This is our last chance!"

"I don't know what else to do!"

Headstrong cursed Bobtail under his breath, then shouted, "All sparrows to me!"

The Winged Regiment followed Headstrong away from the park.

Surt fell in next to Gunlad and took command of the birds of prey. "Finish them!" the peregrine screamed.

"Wake up!" Loki yelled. Ragtag and Tattler awoke with a start and jumped to their feet. They could tell it was midmorning from the position of the sun in the sky.

The ferry was approaching Boston. From their vantage point atop the ship, the birds watched as the Winged Regiment swooped across the Charlestown Navy Yard, over the USS *Constitution*, and into the North End. Behind them rose a cloud of angry raptors.

"What's Bobtail doing?" Tattler yelled. "They weren't supposed to attack until noon!"

"Come on!" Ragtag said, taking flight. Tattler and Loki quickly followed.

"What's our plan?" Tattler asked as they skimmed over the harbor.

Ragtag didn't respond. A sinking feeling came over him as he realized he didn't have one. He had hoped to arrive in time to prevent Bobtail's attack. He'd had a vague idea of begging the clan leaders for forgiveness and pleading with them to flee the city.

But none of that mattered now. As the birds approached the waterfront, they could see the sparrows regrouping on a ledge atop the Custom House Tower. Ragtag pumped his wings and climbed toward it.

Gini flew fast and low through the streets of Boston. She headed straight for the Common, no longer caring whether the birds of prey found the Feathered Alliance's secret base.

Blue Feather, Bragi, Kittiwook, and Blackcap greeted her when she arrived beneath the bridge. The clan leaders had watched the Winged Regiment being pursued by the raptors and were desperate for news.

"What happened?" Blue Feather asked. "The surprise attack—"

"It was a trick," Gini blurted out as soon as she had caught her breath. "The birds of prey knew we were coming!"

"Bobtail . . . Is he . . ." Blue Feather's voice trailed off.

"I don't know," Gini said. "There were raptors everywhere! The Winged Regiment is being slaughtered."

The pigeons wailed as Blackcap jumped forward. "You're Bobtail's second-in-command. What are you doing back here?"

"I can't fight them!" Gini cried. "They're too strong. They're too powerful!"

"You ran away!" the chickadee accused. "You ran and left the others to die!"

"No!" Bragi interrupted. "It was good Gini ran. Better to run and live!"

"Yes, yes," the pigeons chanted. "Run and live! Run and live!"

"Quiet, you cowards," Blackcap yelled, then addressed Kittiwook and Blue Feather. "The Winged Regiment needs help. Even though we're not warriors, I say we fight anyway!"

"I'm with you," Kittiwook declared.

"Round everyone up and get them in the air!" Blue Feather shouted to the clan leaders. "It's time we all made a stand."

Bragi watched as the clan leaders took flight and headed in different directions. A feeling of shame washed over her. She realized that Surt had tricked her and she had fallen for it. Because of her, the Winged Regiment, if not the entire Feathered Alliance, was about to be destroyed.

"What do we do?" one of her pigeons asked.

"Let's run away," another suggested.

"Yes, yes," a third replied. "Run and live!"

"Run and live!" they began to chorus.

"No!" Bragi declared so loudly that even she was taken aback. The other pigeons bobbed their heads and blinked. Bragi's shame had turned to anger. Yes, she was terrified, but so were the others. If they were willing to risk their lives and fight, then so would she.

"What do you mean, no?" a pigeon asked.

"We're going to fight!" Bragi declared.

"Fight?" echoed a dumbstruck pigeon. "How? We're just pigeons."

"Cowardly pigeons!" they all howled.

"Cowardly pigeons would never have carried Bobtail's message to the sparrows," Bragi replied. "We're only cowards because we think we are!"

"But we can't fight," one of her flock protested. "What can we do?"

"Our strength is in our numbers," Bragi said, and took to the air. "Come on! I don't know about you, but I'm tired of being a cowardly pigeon!"

"Wait for me!" another pigeon cried, and hurried after her. One by one, the rest of the flock followed because there is nothing more terrifying to a pigeon than to be left behind.

Atop the Custom House Tower, the exhausted sparrows crowded around Bobtail and Headstrong. In the distance, they could see the birds of prey regrouping over the waterfront, preparing for their final assault.

"They'll be here in minutes!" Headstrong said.

"What do we do?" a sparrow asked.

"We can't fight them all," another declared.

"What are your orders?" Headstrong asked Bobtail.

A ripple of discontent ran through the troops when Bobtail didn't reply. The swallow was trembling and seemed disoriented.

"Snap out of it!" Headstrong said. "Ragtag left you in command. What are your orders? What do we do?"

"We—we—" Bobtail stammered.

"We fight!" Ragtag yelled as he landed on the ledge next to them, followed by Tattler and Loki.

"Ragtag! Tattler!" Headstrong shouted with joy.

"What's happened?" Ragtag asked. "You weren't supposed to attack until noon!"

"You can thank Bobtail for that," a sparrow said.

"Never mind that now," Headstrong said quickly. "The raptors will be here any second. Ragtag, where's your eagle?"

"I'm sorry," Ragtag said, bowing his head. "I failed. I couldn't convince him to return with us."

A moan of despair went through the birds.

"Then it's over," Bobtail said. "We might as well give up."

"No!" Ragtag yelled. He glanced at the birds of prey heading in their direction. They had only seconds.

"Listen to me!" Ragtag said as he took to the air and hovered over the sparrows. "This city is my home. This city is *our* home. Our nests are here, our children are here, our elders are here. I'm tired of running away!"

"But, Ragtag," Bobtail protested, "we'll be killed if we stay and fight. There's no way we can win."

"If that's my fate, then so be it. Hoogol fought and died for his freedom. I would rather die the way he did than wait to be hunted down and killed like a cowardly mouse hiding in some hole!"

Ragtag suddenly folded his wings and plunged toward the raptors.

"Has he gone mad?" Headstrong asked.

"Definitely," Tattler replied, and followed him down.

"Well, what are we waiting for?" Headstrong shouted. The birds exchanged startled glances, then cheered loudly and followed him as he dropped toward the raptors. Only Loki stayed behind.

"You fools," the crow muttered. "This is nothing but suicide." He hopped from foot to foot, torn by conflicting emotions. He didn't want to admit that he had grown attached to Ragtag, and even to Tattler, despite her feelings about him.

"You're all fools," Loki said again. "And I must be the biggest fool of them all," he added as he dove off the ledge and hurried to join the fight.

Gunlad

Loki's Redemption

Ragtag's wings were pressed close to his body. His eyes had shrunk to slits and his claws were tightly curled. Beside him flew Tattler, and behind her were more than a hundred sparrows. Ragtag was happy Tattler was at his side. He felt a strange sense of calm as they dove toward the birds of prey. The uncertainty and worry about finding Baldur was gone, and he no longer feared the last battle. His only wish was to take as many raptors with him as he could.

"Ready?" Ragtag shouted.

"Now!" Tattler yelled. Ragtag and Tattler twisted their bodies so they were flying stomach to stomach. The two birds locked claws and pulled themselves together, doubling their weight and size.

They aimed for a peregrine falcon, hoping it was Surt, and slammed into him at full speed. The force of the impact knocked the smaller birds senseless. Ragtag found himself wheeling through the sky, the buildings spinning around him in a dizzying blur. He snapped out of it and righted himself just in time to catch a glimpse of a lifeless falcon hurtling to the ground.

"We did it!" Tattler chirped.

Above him, the Winged Regiment plummeted from the sky. Ragtag watched as sparrow after sparrow dive-bombed the birds of prey. Some missed their marks altogether; others struck but with such force that they too lost their lives.

A horrible screech came from somewhere above him. Ragtag caught sight of Surt swooping through the sparrows, knocking them from the sky, one by one. They had targeted the wrong falcon.

"Tattler!" Ragtag cried in despair.

"I see him," Tattler yelled back. "Better luck next time."

Before Ragtag could reply, he found himself lost in a sea of flashing talons. Cries and screams of injured and dying birds filled the air. Feathers filled the sky, making it almost impossible to see where he was flying.

"Ragtag!" a voice yelled. The swallow's blood ran cold as Surt forced his way through the ranks of the Winged Regiment. "Ragtag, show yourself!"

Ragtag felt a surge of anger and hate. He banked hard and was about to answer the challenge when Loki flew up beside him.

"Don't be a fool!" the crow said. "He's baiting you. If you fall, the battle is over." Loki darted away as a pair of sharpies caught sight of him and gave chase.

Loki's right, Ragtag thought, as he maneuvered to attack a kestrel from behind. The raptor beat off the attack, and Ragtag dove away.

"Where's Tattler?" Ragtag asked a pair of sparrows. He had lost track of her in the chaos.

"No idea!" one of the sparrows yelled. Before Ragtag could respond, they were gone.

We need help, Ragtag thought as he nipped at the tail feathers of a black-hawk who had set his sights on Bobtail. The black-hawk retreated, and Bobtail was able to escape.

A sudden cheer rose into the air. Something red flashed past Ragtag and collided with a hawk. A flock of cardinals had joined the fray! Ragtag darted away as the sparrows sang their joy. A loud *"keew-keew"* came from above as two dozen seagulls swooped down.

Ragtag's spirits soared. Finches, blue jays, starlings, and robins were approaching from all directions. Word had gone out that the Winged Regiment needed help, and birds from all over the city were responding.

"Kill them all!" Surt yelled as he savagely slashed at the newcomers.

Loki spotted Hugin and Munin attacking a pair of starlings beneath him. He climbed into the sky, then wrapped his wings around himself and dove toward the sisters. At the last minute, he banked, his claws slashing Hugin's tail. The merlin yelped in surprise and spun out of control.

Beneath the birds, humans had stopped to watch the battle unfolding over their heads. The crowd gasped as Hugin plunged toward the ground. She desperately spread her wings to control her descent, but it was too late. The merlin smashed into a hot dog stand at over fifty miles an hour.

Munin watched her twin fall and hurtled toward the crow, determined to avenge her sister.

"Come on, you overstuffed goose!" Loki taunted as he saw her approach. He bolted away from the battle, zoomed over the docks and across the harbor.

"Stupid crow!" Munin shouted. "You can't outfly me over the water."

"I wasn't planning to," Loki yelled as his eyes fell on a tugboat chugging around a freighter. He banked hard and flew parallel to the freighter's hull. This has to be timed just right, he thought.

"I'm going to take your body back to Surt as a tribute!" Munin said as she came within striking distance.

"You'll have to catch me first," Loki shouted, then dove into the waves. Munin shot past him. The startled merlin looked over her shoulder, stunned to see Loki emerge from the water.

"Heads up!" Loki cackled. Munin glanced forward just as the tugboat rounded the freighter's bow. She collided with it headfirst, then dropped into the sea and sank out of sight.

Ragtag joined Bobtail and Headstrong in the air. Beneath them, what was left of the Winged Regiment continued to attack Surt and the raptors, but even with the help of the other clans, they couldn't turn the tide of battle.

"Ragtag, look!" Bobtail said. A dark cloud was approaching from the south. The others saw it too, and a feeling of uneasiness spread among the birds.

"More raptors?" Headstrong asked.

"No," Ragtag declared with relief. "It's the crows! The crows are joining the fight!"

"And it's about time," Loki called as he zoomed past them.

Garm hurtled down from the sky along with forty other crows and collided with the angry raptors.

The Winged Regiment had a renewed surge of strength and rushed forward to re-engage the birds of prey. Ragtag was about to join them when a familiar voice called to him. He braked hard and almost collided with Blue Feather.

"Mom!" Ragtag yelled with a mixture of happiness and concern. "What are you doing here?"

"Helping out, of course!"

"Mom—my eagle, I couldn't—"

"Don't worry," Blue Feather interrupted. "Tattler told me. You tried, and that's what counts."

"But it's not enough," Ragtag said as he watched the battle unfold. The sheer number of birds who had taken to the sky to fight the empire was breathtaking, yet Ragtag knew they couldn't win.

"Look on the bright side!" Blue Feather said as she dodged an osprey. "You brought the entire city together. Even the crows! Not even Hoogol could have done that. They're fighting for you, Ragtag!"

A short distance away, Tattler spotted Gunlad's distinctive tail.

"Come on!" she yelled to a pair of sparrows. The three birds collided simultaneously with the hawk. Gunlad squawked in pain as Tattler slashed at his wings. He shook off the other sparrows and set his sights on the leader of the Winged Regiment.

"Tattler!" Gunlad roared.

Tattler bolted away, weaving through the buildings lining the waterfront. She could hear the flapping of Gunlad's wings behind her.

She banked and dove for the Custom House Tower, spiraling down around it with breathtaking speed. Let's see him try to follow me now, she thought. Tattler reached the ground and looked back. Her heart fell when she saw that Gunlad had not only matched her maneuver but had closed the gap between them.

Tattler forced her exhausted wings to a new effort. She shot down State Street, then Tremont, desperately looking for a place to hide. In the distance lay the Boston Common. She headed for it, hoping she could lose herself amid the trees or take cover under the bridge.

Gunlad kept up his pursuit as Tattler entered the Public Garden and zoomed over the lake. The hawk finally caught up to her, and his talons raked her left wing.

Tattler cried out and dropped fast, her wounded wing trailing uselessly behind her. She crashed onto the bank of the lake and skidded to a stop.

"Long live the Feathered Alliance!" Tattler yelled as the hawk swooped down to strike.

There was a sudden flash of black feathers as Loki plunged out of the sky and collided with Gunlad. The two birds toppled to the ground and rolled end over end through the grass.

Gunlad leaped to his feet, talons slashing. Loki fluttered into the air and landed on top of him, sinking his claws into Gunlad's wings as he viciously pecked at the raptor's face.

Gunlad forced Loki back toward the wrought-iron fence surrounding the Common. Loki slammed into it hard, his breath knocked out of him.

"You fool!" Gunlad spat. "A crow is no match for a red-tailed hawk!"

Loki fluttered back into the air. Gunlad hurtled forward and struck him from behind. Loki twisted, his claws grappling with the hawk's talons, their wings tangled together. The two birds hung for a moment in midair, then dropped toward the fence.

Tattler watched in horror as Gunlad struck the fence first, with Loki atop him. The hawk shrieked horribly, then fell silent. Surt's heir was impaled on the iron spikes.

Loki dropped to the ground and lay motionless as Tattler limped over to him. The crow's feathers were covered with blood.

"Loki?" said Tattler.

"Sorry I was late," the crow gasped. "I tried catching up with you over the waterfront, but you were too fast. Gunlad—is he . . ."

"He's dead," Tattler said, averting her eyes from the body.

"Whoever would've thought I had it in me?" Loki said as he struggled for breath. He was losing blood fast.

"Loki, don't talk."

"Won't make much difference now," Loki whispered.

"I hope you'll think better of crows in the future. Perhaps . . ." Loki's voice trailed off.

"Loki?" Tattler said as she moved closer. "Loki?"

Loki was dead.

Garm

The Greatest Symphony

T his is suicide!" Bobtail yelled to Ragtag.
"We've lost more than fifty sparrows," Headstrong added. "Even with the help of the crows, the raptors are just too strong out in the open!"

"Then we won't fight them in the open," Ragtag yelled back. "Order the brigades to split up. Try to draw the raptors to the ground. We'll have the advantage!"

Bobtail and Headstrong nodded and darted away.

"Follow me!" Ragtag shouted as he spotted Blackcap and his brothers. They zoomed over Faneuil Hall and swooped down into Quincy Market, the raptors on their tails.

On the ground, dozens of humans were sitting at tables or shopping for food, when suddenly more than two hundred birds flooded the market. Tables and stalls were overturned, fruits and vegetables flying in all directions.

"Use the humans as shields!" Headstrong yelled, and dropped toward the ground with two dozen other birds.

They zoomed around the stalls, dodging the startled humans and nipping at the enraged raptors.

Surt hissed in frustration. The larger, bulkier birds of prey were having a hard time keeping up. The falcon emperor watched as an osprey tried to follow a sparrow's hairpin turn. The sparrow darted away as the osprey flew headfirst into a wall.

Headstrong bolted away from a kestrel, laughing as he swooped under a picnic table. A harrier screamed at him and gave chase, but its longer wings clipped the table posts and sent it careening into a garbage can.

Kittiwook took shelter next to an overturned chair. When a pair of hawks zoomed past chasing a band of sparrows, she took a deep breath and imitated the call of a peregrine. *"Keeek-keeek-kek-kek!"*

The hawks came to an abrupt stop in midair.

"You fools!" Kittiwook yelled, in Surt's voice. "You're flying the wrong way!" The hawks backtracked as Kittiwook laughed.

A few feet away, Ragtag and the chickadees were being chased by a goshawk. The raptor swooped down with his talons outstretched, but Garm suddenly collided with the bird of prey. The goshawk squawked in pain and retreated.

"Thanks," Ragtag said, landing safely on an awning.

The crow nodded and flew off with the chickadees. Ragtag stopped to catch his breath. So far his plan was working. Closer to the ground, the birds of the city could outmaneuver the raptors and coordinate their attacks instead of fighting them one-on-one, evening the odds.

On the opposite side of the market, Surt landed on a table. The falcon's keen eyes quickly found what he was searching for.

"Ragtag!" Surt screamed, and launched himself from the table.

Ragtag's blood ran cold when he spotted the falcon emperor headed toward him, along with four sharpies.

"Get out of here!" Bobtail yelled. Ragtag bolted away. Headstrong and a pair of sparrows fell in beside him, and together they rocketed down Court Street.

"Can't you fly any faster?" Headstrong yelled. "They're gaining on us!"

Ragtag looked behind him. His stomach tightened when he saw that Surt and the raptors were indeed closing the gap.

"I have an idea!" Ragtag called back. "Follow me!" He banked sharply and headed into the middle of the street, followed by the sparrows and the raptors. Cars rushed at them, horns honking. The birds whipped around the vehicles, dodging left and right.

Surt spread his wings as a truck barreled toward him, soaring over it in the nick of time. The sharpies followed him, gliding over the traffic. The larger birds of prey couldn't risk flying between the cars.

"You call this a plan?" Headstrong shouted to Ragtag as he narrowly missed slamming into a bus. "We're going to get pulverized if we stay down here!"

Ragtag forced himself to remain calm while he flew under a car and emerged safely on the opposite side. He knew Headstrong was right. If they stayed where they were, the humans' vehicles would do the raptors' job for them. Making up his mind, he quickly took an opening that led out of traffic.

The raptors cackled with glee as they watched their prey leave the relative safety of the cars. They swooped down and picked up the chase.

Ragtag and the sparrows did everything they could to shake their pursuers, making hair-raising turns through backyards, skimming over fences, through trees, and under bushes. But try as they might, the raptors stuck to their tails like glue.

"We can't lose them!" Headstrong shouted over the wind.

"Split up and try to take some of them with you!" Ragtag shouted, hoping it would be easier to escape the raptors if they became separated in an unfamiliar city. Headstrong nodded and darted across an intersection while Ragtag soared down Boylston Street, instinctively heading for home.

"Follow them, but leave Ragtag for me!" Surt ordered the sharpies.

Ragtag pushed his wings to their breaking point. He zoomed over a high-rise, the falcon following so closely the two birds were almost touching.

"You're tiring, little bird!" Surt laughed at the swallow struggling to maintain his speed. "It's only a matter of time."

Ragtag knew he was right. So this is where it ends, he thought as he entered Copley Square. He had fought and risked his life these last few days for nothing. He would be caught and killed, and so would all the other birds fighting for their freedom. In the end, the Talon Empire would win, as it always did.

One last desperate idea sprang to mind when Ragtag's eyes fell upon a partially opened window that led into the Boston Public Library. Having been raised in the city, he knew the dangers of glass—and how often birds mistook it for open air. Would Surt, who had lived his entire life in the country, make the same mistake?

Ragtag zoomed across the street at top speed, not stopping to think that the slightest miscalculation on his part would mean certain death. With the window rushing toward him, the swallow flattened his body and slid through. He fluttered his wings to brake his speed, bounced off a table, and skidded to a stop on the floor.

A shadow fell over the glass. Then, a split second later, it exploded into shards. Surt had indeed mistaken the glass for air. But instead of knocking him unconscious, the falcon's weight and speed had simply shattered the window.

Ragtag took flight while a bloodied and enraged Surt crashed to the floor. Startled humans scrambled out of their seats as the falcon chased the smaller bird through the library.

The swallow banked and darted across the main reading room and down a marble staircase. But he was forced to spread his wings upon reaching a dead end. Rows of books were stacked from floor to ceiling. Landing on a shelf, he backed himself into a corner as Surt entered the room.

"Where are you?" the falcon roared. "Why is the leader of the great Feathered Alliance hiding like a common rat?"

Ragtag hid behind a thick hardcover and tried to keep as still as possible while Surt fluttered from one stack of books to the next.

"So much for the great Ragtag," the falcon taunted. "While you cower and hide, my raptors are destroying your clans. Is this your idea of leadership? Is this how you define courage?"

He's goading you, Ragtag thought as he heard a shuffle of feathers over his head. Surt was walking over the books on the shelf directly above him.

"You're a coward, Ragtag!" Surt yelled. "Just like your predecessor. Oh, yes, Bergelmir told me all about Hoogol, how he fled and hid while his father and the Council of Nine were slaughtered. And now, history repeats itself. You sit here hiding, afraid to face me, while outside my raptors are ripping apart what's left of your clans!"

"Hoogol wasn't a coward!" Ragtag squeaked. "You are! You're nothing but a bully!"

Both birds whirled as a janitor appeared waving a broom. Ragtag bolted around the human. Surt followed, his wings smashing into the man's face on the way out.

Ragtag shot like a bullet through an open door that led outside, and Surt was instantly behind him. This time Ragtag couldn't escape. With a triumphant yell, Surt snatched him out of the air.

Gripping Ragtag tightly in his talons, the peregrine falcon carried him across Boylston Street. The swallow glimpsed a crowd of humans entering the Old South Church just as Surt spread his wings and landed in the belfry.

"It's over!" he declared.

Ragtag closed his eyes and waited for the final blow. He thought of all the birds he had let down. He thought of his mother, Blue Feather, and his brother, Bobtail. He thought of Tattler and Headstrong, Bragi and Kittiwook, Blackcap and Loki. He thought of Proud Beak and Hoogol, and was overwhelmed by sadness.

"Your alliance thinks of you as a symbol," Surt gloated as he loomed over the swallow. "Indeed you shall be—a symbol representing the fate of all those who dare to stand against the Talon Empire." Surt squeezed his talons. "Open your eyes, Ragtag. I want my face to be the last one you see before you die."

Ragtag opened his eyes, but it wasn't Surt's face that made his heart race. An image of the crowd of humans entering the church below suddenly came to him. He knew he had one last chance if he could just keep Surt from killing him for a few more moments.

"You'll never hold the city!" Ragtag declared defiantly.

"Is that so?" Surt laughed, taking the bait. "And who will stop us?"

"The humans!" Ragtag answered.

Surt hesitated and the swallow quickly continued. "Why do you think no birds of prey live here? They're afraid of the humans!"

"You're lying," Surt said. "Humans don't care what happens in our world. They care only about themselves."

"No, I'm telling the truth. I was friends with an eagle once, and his fate will be yours. You'll be captured and locked away! The great Surt—leader of the Talon Empire—will live the rest of his life alone in a cage. Do you know what happens to a bird of prey when he's locked in a cage too long? He grows to like it. He forgets what it means to be free!"

Surt laughed. "You tell a good story, Ragtag, but some-how I doubt it. In any case, no matter what the future may hold—you won't be around to see it."

Surt raised a talon and prepared to end the young swal-low's life. But at that moment, a tremendous noise echoed through the belfry. The peregrine falcon stumbled back at the peal of the bell. Ragtag, who was accustomed to the sound, used his last ounce of strength to jump up and fly out.

Surt tried to follow but was off balance and staggering as the bell continued to peal. The sound was deafening, and the vibrations knocked the peregrine off his feet. Surt screamed, burying his head beneath his wings in a vain attempt to drown out the noise.

Finally, the bell fell silent; the last vibrations died away. Ragtag looked up from where he lay on the ledge outside the belfry. Surt slowly climbed to his feet. The falcon emperor had a crazed look. He slowly lurched forward, his talons rak-ing the belfry's floor.

"Ragtag!" Headstrong shouted as he shot overhead and slammed into the falcon. Surt snarled and swiped at him.

"Ragtag!" Bobtail yelled, and struck the falcon from the rear.

"Cheereek! Cheereek!"

Surt whirled in shock at the sound of Bergelmir's scream. Kittiwook laughed and flew forward to attack.

"Ragtag! Ragtag!" The belfry was suddenly filled with birds, claws scratching and beaks snapping.

A pair of black wings flashed past Ragtag. For a second, he thought it was Loki, but it was Garm. He was followed by crow after crow, all of them converging to mob the falcon emperor.

Surt's talons flashed. Feathers filled the air. The birds continued to dart about, attacking the falcon.

"Brave pigeons! Brave pigeons!" Bragi shouted, fluttering into the belfry along with her flock. The pigeons clucked loudly and began to peck at Surt.

Ragtag watched in amazement as gulls, finches, blue jays, and robins dragged Surt down and buried him under a mass of wings and feathers.

And then it was over. Ragtag painfully got to his feet and hopped forward as the birds backed away from Surt. The falcon emperor lay dead on the floor of the belfry.

"I don't believe it," Ragtag said.

"We did it!" Bobtail yelled.

"Surt's dead!" Headstrong roared. "Long live the Feathered Alliance!"

A great cheer went up from the birds. The Feathered Alliance had joined together with the crows and accomplished the impossible.

"Surt's dead," Ragtag said to himself. "The falcon emperor's dead." He repeated it over and over, not believing his own eyes, expecting at any moment to be awakened from a dream. Watching the celebrating birds, he suddenly felt uneasy. He remembered what Hoogol had told him—the Talon Empire was more than just one ruler.

A scream from outside echoed through the belfry and the joyous mood suddenly died. Everyone turned in shock to see a mass of raptors approaching from the north. Hawks, ospreys, harriers, and kestrels were zooming toward them.

"We're finished," Bobtail whispered. "We don't have the strength or numbers to win."

"At least we'll take some of them with us," Ragtag replied.

"Indeed we will," Garm said.

The other birds nodded. They spread their wings and took to the air, knowing it would be for the last time. Surt's death had been an empty victory. The clans were exhausted and wounded. They all knew they had no chance against the power of the remaining birds of prey. But they would fight.

Ragtag rose into the air and headed toward the advancing raptors. Gulls, pigeons, finches, blue jays, robins, and crows fell in behind him.

The two armies flew faster and faster and grew closer and closer. Just as they were about to meet, the raptors suddenly spread their wings to brake their speed.

The birds of the city looked up in astonishment to see seven bald eagles plummet from the clouds. Beaks snapped and talons clashed against talons as the massive birds tore through the ranks of the empire.

Baldur emerged from the melee and shouted, "What are you waiting for? Do you expect us to do *all* the work?"

"Come on!" Ragtag yelled, his heart leaping with joy.

A mighty cheer arose from the birds of the city as the eagles decimated their opponents. With renewed energy, the clans zoomed forward and joined the fight.

The tide of battle quickly turned against the raptors. With their emperor dead and nobody to lead them, the remaining members of the Talon Empire scattered and fled the fury of Baldur and the other eagles. Ragtag shouted triumphantly at the top of his lungs and the cry was quickly picked up by the other clans.

Down in the streets, startled humans looked up in wonder as the birds of the city erupted into song. It was a symphony greater than any they had ever heard.

Where's Ragtag? Blue Feather wondered as she gazed down from the roof of the John Hancock Tower. A gust of wind hit her and she fearfully hopped back.

She had never liked heights. The belfry of the Old South Church had always made her nervous, and now she was so much higher. Ragtag had decided that the top of the skyscraper would be the new headquarters for the Feathered Alliance.

Oh, well, Blue Feather thought, admiring the view. It's just this one time. She had already resigned as leader of the swallows. Bobtail had eagerly taken her place, and was now second-in-command to Ragtag. It was a job he would enjoy far more than she ever had.

Blue Feather crossed over to the other clan leaders. Gulls, pigeons, finches, blue jays, and robins were gathered, their eyes on the six eagles sitting on the roof's edge. The eagles were grooming themselves and looked rather bored. Blue Feather had already forgotten their names, although she knew that the larger one was Baldur's mate, Freya, and the other five were Freya's brothers and sisters.

Ragtag and Baldur had been scouring the city since yesterday's victory, looking for any stragglers from the empire.

Blue Feather hoped her son would return soon. Even though she knew the eagles were friendly, they still made her nervous. She had never seen birds so *big*.

"Any sign of him?" Tattler asked as she limped forward. The sparrow's wing was mending, but it would still be weeks before she could fly. In the meantime, she was hitching rides on the backs of some of the larger gulls.

"No," Blue Feather sighed.

"How typical," Bobtail said as he joined them. "You would think that now that Ragtag's the leader of the Feathered Alliance, he would bother to show up on time for council meetings."

Blue Feather stifled a laugh. Bobtail was beginning to remind her of Proud Beak.

"To be fair," Tattler said, "Hoogol never used to arrive on time, either."

The birds fell silent at the mention of the great horned owl. It had been three days since his death, but they had been so preoccupied fighting the Talon Empire that they hadn't had time to mourn. Now that the raptors had fled the city, however, the birds' thoughts were turning more and more to Hoogol, Proud Beak, Loki, and all the others who had lost their lives. Headstrong alone had lost five cousins. They had won the war, but they had paid a terrible price.

Blue Feather looked out from her perch. The sun was high overhead, and not a single cloud marred the sky. The future seemed bright and full of promise. "I wish Hoogol were here to see this."

The birds nodded in agreement.

A sudden *"caw-caw"* attracted their attention. Bobtail watched uneasily as Garm and a dozen crows landed on the far side of the roof. There had been an uneasy truce between the crows and the alliance in the hours since the Talon Empire had been routed, but there was still a great deal of mistrust on both sides.

"I don't know why they have to be here," Bobtail complained. "I mean, this is supposed to be an official council meeting. Crows aren't allowed."

"Ragtag asked them to attend," Blue Feather replied.

Just then, Blackcap and his brothers chirped excitedly from their posts near the roof's edge. "Look, everyone!" Blackcap cried. "Here they come!"

Ragtag clung to Baldur's back as they soared over Copley Square. He still couldn't believe the eagle had returned. Baldur had been true to his word and kept his promises to both Ragtag and his mate. As soon as he had been reunited with Freya, he had convinced her and her family to return with him to the city.

"How do you like it?" Baldur asked as they soared past the Boston Public Library.

"I've never flown so fast in my life!" Ragtag yelled as the wind pressed back his feathers. He gasped in awe as the eagle beat his powerful wings. Together they climbed the nearly eight hundred feet to the top of the John Hancock Tower in a matter of seconds.

Beneath them, Ragtag could see the clan leaders. He

waited impatiently while Baldur glided down to the roof. This was one council meeting he didn't want to miss.

"Bobtail, Blue Feather, Tattler!" Ragtag shouted as he hurried over to them. He was quickly surrounded by birds. "Sorry I'm late."

"Well?" the crowd asked with bated breath.

"I'm happy to report there's no sign of the raptors. The birds of prey have fled the city!"

"Is it truly over, then?" Kittiwook asked. "Are they gone for good?"

"It's unlikely they'll bother you again," Baldur said. "It's hard for raptors to get along with one another even in the best of times. With no leader to guide them, they'll probably scatter and go their separate ways. And even if they do manage to regroup, I doubt they'll be bold enough to return, now that they know your alliance is under the protection of eagles. No, I think it's safe to say that the Talon Empire is gone for good."

A cheer went up from the birds. Ragtag caught sight of the crows standing on the far side of the roof and suddenly felt sad. Tattler had told him about Loki. A hush fell on the crowd as Ragtag crossed over to them.

"I want to thank you for your help," Ragtag said to Garm. "We wouldn't have been able to defeat Surt without you."

Garm bowed his head.

"I'm sorry about Loki," Ragtag continued. "I wish he were here."

"I am an old crow," Garm said. "I've seen many battles and watched countless friends perish. I, too, feel sorry about Loki. His death feels empty and without meaning."

"Only if we allow it to be," Ragtag replied, and took a deep breath. "We came together to defeat a common enemy. Why return to our old ways? We have a chance to make Hoogol's and Loki's deaths count for something. I say let's put aside our differences! Let's unite *all* the clans of the city. Will the crows join the Feathered Alliance?"

The clan leaders froze. Bobtail stared at his brother in surprise. Nobody had expected this. Even Garm seemed taken aback. The old crow cocked his head to one side and peered at Ragtag.

"You're full of surprises. I'll say one thing about you, Ragtag. You are a worthy successor to Hoogol."

"Well?" Ragtag asked. "Will you join us?"

"Upon Loki's death, the leadership of the crows passed to me. Yet this is not a decision I can make on my own."

Ragtag nodded and watched as Garm returned to his clan. Instantly the swallow was mobbed by the other birds.

"Have you gone mad?" Kittiwook demanded. "It'll never work!"

"She's right," Bragi said. "It's one thing to have a truce with the crows, quite another to have them as members of the alliance."

"Heaven help us!" the pigeons wailed.

Bobtail shook his head. "Poor Ragtag, always the dreamer. If Hoogol couldn't make peace between the crows and the Feathered Alliance, what makes you think you can?"

Ragtag didn't respond. He waited anxiously until Garm flew back. "Well?"

"Your youth and optimism are infectious, Ragtag. Alas,

old prejudices die hard. I wish I could give you better news, but the crows cannot accept your offer.

"However," Garm added as Ragtag slumped, "just because we don't join the Feathered Alliance today doesn't mean we can't build on what's been started here. Who knows? Perhaps in time even old prejudices will fade. Until then, I've volunteered to act as an ambassador to your alliance, if you'll have me."

"With pleasure," Ragtag replied, then addressed the clan leaders. "Who will represent us to the crows?"

The birds shifted uncomfortably and averted their eyes.

"I will," Tattler said suddenly.

Everyone watched in surprise as she limped forward. There was a murmur from the crows. Garm looked at Tattler for a long time without responding. Then the old crow bowed his head. "We welcome you."

"Hoogol would've been proud of us," Ragtag said. "I think today marks the beginning of a bright future for the birds of the city."

"Indeed it does," Baldur agreed. "And now, little Ragtag, it is time for us to say farewell."

"What?" Ragtag cried. The idea that the eagles might leave hadn't occurred to him.

"We have a new home across the Great Water," Baldur said. He indicated the device on his leg. "And as I'm sure you're aware, our caretakers get rather worried when we're away too long."

"But we need you!" Ragtag pleaded. "Baldur, please don't leave!"

"I'm afraid we must. Besides, I'm not convinced you need us as much as you think. After all, we didn't bring down Surt. We merely helped clean up the mess."

The eagle lowered his head and gazed at the swallow. "You have the heart of an eagle," Baldur said quietly. "As long as you and your friends stick together, I don't think there's anything you can't overcome."

Freya and her family impatiently stretched their wings. Baldur joined them at the edge of the roof. "Farewell, little Ragtag!"

"Goodbye, Baldur!" Ragtag shouted. "I'll never forget you!"

"Nor I you," Baldur replied. "You will always have a friend among the eagles."

And with that, the eagles launched themselves from the top of the skyscraper. They circled once, then headed out over the harbor. Ragtag watched as they grew smaller and finally disappeared altogether.

"Well, let's not stand around here all day," Bobtail said, tapping his foot. "We're long overdue for a council meeting. Do you know how much work we have to do? We'll be lucky if we finish before nightfall."

The birds groaned and followed him to the center of the roof. Ragtag stayed behind, his eyes on the sky where the eagles had vanished. Tattler hopped up to him. "You okay, Ragtag?"

"Yeah," Ragtag replied. "I was just thinking of Hoogol."

"He would have been proud of you," Tattler said quietly. "I know I am. You did well, Ragtag. Not bad for a swallow. Not bad at all."

ACKNOWLEDGMENTS

Thanks to Sukhwinder Singh, Daniel Skoumal, and Chris Donaldson. Thanks also to Jan de Bont and Jessika Borsiczky, for providing the initial encouragement to write this story. And a special thank you to Jennifer Wingertzahn and the entire staff at Clarion Books. Without them, Ragtag would never have taken flight.